The Penguin Poets

The Penguin Book of
Modern African Poetry

The Penguin Book of Modern African Poetry

Edited by
Gerald Moore and Ulli Beier

Third Edition

Penguin Books

PENGUIN BOOKS

Published by the Penguin Group
Penguin Books Ltd, 27 Wrights Lane, London W8 5TZ, England
Penguin Books USA Inc., 375 Hudson Street, New York, New York 10014, USA
Penguin Books Australia Ltd, Ringwood, Victoria, Australia
Penguin Books Canada Ltd, 10 Alcorn Avenue, Toronto, Ontario, Canada M4V 3B2
Penguin Books (NZ) Ltd, 182–190 Wairau Road, Auckland 10, New Zealand

Penguin Books Ltd, Registered Offices: Harmondsworth, Middlesex, England

Modern Poetry from Africa first published 1963
Second edition 1968
Third edition reissued as *The Penguin Book of Modern African Poetry* 1984
10 9 8

Printed in England by Clays Ltd, St Ives plc
Set in Times

Contents

Introduction   19

POEMS

ANGOLA   *Augustinho Neto* (1922–79)

                Farewell at the Moment of
                Parting   27
                African Poem   28
                Kinaxixi   29
                The Grieved Lands   29

                Antonio Jacinto (b.1924)

                Monangamba   31
                Poem of Alienation   32
                Letter from a Contract Worker   35

                Costa Andrade (b.1936)

                Fourth Poem of a Canto of
                Accusation   37

                Ngudia Wendel (b.1940)

                We Shall Return, Luanda   38

                Jofre Rocha (b.1941)

                Poem of Return   40

                Ruy Duarte de Carvalho (b.1941)

                I Come from a South   41

BENIN (DAHOMEY)   *Emile Ologoudou* (b.1935)

Vespers   45
Liberty   46

CAMEROUN   *Simon Mpondo* (b.1935?)

The Season of the Rains   49

Mbella Sonne Dipoko (b.1936)

Our Life   51
Pain   51
Exile   52
A Poem of Villeneuve St
Georges   52
From My Parisian Diary   54

Patrice Kayo (b.1942)

Song of the Initiate   55
War   56

CAPE VERDE ISLANDS *Onésima Silveira* (b.1936)

A Different Poem   59

CONGO REPUBLIC   *Tchicaya U Tam'si* (b.1931)

Three poems from *Feu de
Brousse* (1957):

Brush-fire   63
Dance to the Amulets   63
A Mat to Weave   64

Four poems from *Epitomé*
(1962):

I was naked   66
What do I want with a thousand
stars   66
You must be from my country   67
The Scorner   68

Two poems from *Le Ventre* (1964):

I myself will be the stage   68
I tear at my belly   69

From *L'Arc Musical* (1970):

Epitaph   69

Jean-Baptiste Tati-Loutard (b.1939)

Four poems from *Poèmes de la
Mer* (1968):

News of My Mother   70
The Voices   70
Submarine Tombs   71
Pilgrimage to Loango Strand   71

Two poems from *Les Racines
Congolaises* (1968):

Noonday in Immaturity   72
Death and Rebirth   72

Emmanuel Dongala (b.1941)

Fantasy under the Moon   74

GAMBIA   *Lenrie Peters* (b.1932)

Homecoming   77
Song   77
We Have Come Home   78
One Long Jump   79
Parachute Men   81
Isatou Died   82

GHANA   *Ellis Ayitey Komey* (b.1927)

The Change   85
Oblivion   86

                 Kwesi Brew (b.1928)

A Plea for Mercy   87
The Search   88

                 Kofi Awoonor (b.1935)

Songs of Sorrow   89
Song of War   91
The Sea Eats the Land at Home   92

Three poems from *Rediscovery*
(1964):

Lovers' Song   93
The Weaver Bird   93
Easter Dawn   93

From *Night of My Blood* (1971):

At the Gates   94

From *Ride Me, Memory* (1973):

Afro-American Beats III: An
American Memory of Africa   96

From *The House by the Sea* (1978):

The First Circle   97

Atukwei Okai (b.1941)

999 Smiles   99

Kofi Anyidoho (b.1947)

Hero and Thief   103
Soul in Birthwaters: VI Ghosts   104

GUINEA   *Ahmed Tidjani-Cissé* (b.1947)

Home News   107
Of Colours and Shadows   108

IVORY COAST   *Joseph Miezan Bognini* (b.1936)

From *Ce Dur Appel de l'Espoir*
(1960):

My Days Overgrown   113
Earth and Sky   114

Two poems from *Herbe Féconde*
(1973):

We are men of the new world   115
Suddenly an old man   115

Charles Nokan (b.1937)

My Head is Immense   116

KENYA   *Khadambi Asalache* (b.1934)

Death of a Chief   119

KENYA
continued

Jonathan Kariara (b.1935)

A Leopard Lives in a Muu Tree   121

Jared Angira (b.1936)

If   122
The Country of the Dead   123
Manna   124
A Look in the Past   125
Request   126

MADAGASCAR

Jean-Joseph Rabéarivelo (1901–37)

Four poems from
Traduits de la Nuit:

What invisible rat   129
The hide of the black cow   130
She whose eyes   130
The black glassmaker   131

From Presques-songes (1934):

Cactus   132

Flavien Ranaivo (b.1914)

Song of a Young Girl   133
Song of a Common Lover   134

MALAWI

David Rubadiri (b.1930):

An African Thunderstorm   137

Felix Mnthali (b.1933)

My Father   138

The Stranglehold of English Lit.   139
The Celebration   140

Jack Mapanje (b. 1945?)

Before Chilembwe Tree   141
On Being Asked to Write a
Poem for 1979   142
An Elegy for Mangochi
Fishermen   142
At the Metro: Old Irrelevant
Images   143
The Cheerful Girls at Smiller's
Bar, 1971   143

MALI   *Ouologuem Yambo* (b.1940)

When Negro Teeth Speak   147

MAURETANIA   *Oumar Ba* (b.1900)

Justice is Done   151
Familiar Oxen   151
The Ox-Soldier   151
Nobility   152

MAURITIUS   *Edouard Maunick* (b.1931)

Two poems from *Les Maneges de
la Mer* (1964):

Further off is the measured force   155
I love to encounter you   155

MOZAMBIQUE

José Craveiriñha (b.1922)

The Seed is in Me   159
Three Dimensions   160

Noémia de Sousa (b.1927)

Appeal   161
If You Want to Know Me   162

Valente Malangatana (b.1936)

To the Anxious Mother   164
Woman   165

Jorge Rebelo (b.1940)

Poem   166
Poem for a Militant   167

NIGERIA

Gabriel Okara (b.1921)

The Snowflakes Sail Gently
Down   171
The Mystic Drum   172
Adhiambo   173
Spirit of the Wind   174
One Night at Victoria Beach   175

Christopher Okigbo (1932–67)

Seven poems from *Heavensgate*
(1961):

Overture   176
Eyes Watch the Stars   176
Water Maid   177
Sacrifice   178
Passion Flower   178

Lustra   179
Bridge   179

Four poems from *Limits* (1962):

Suddenly becoming talkative   180
For he was a shrub   180
Banks of reed   181
An image insists   182

One poem from *Lament of the Drums* (1964)   183

Two poems from *Distances* (1964):

From flesh into phantom   183
Death lay in ambush   184

From *Come Thunder* (1967):

Come Thunder   186

Wole Soyinka (b.1934)

Telephone Conversation   187

Seven poems from *Idanre & Other Poems* (1967):

Death in the Dawn   188
Massacre, October '66   189
Civilian and Soldier   190
Prisoner   191
Season   192
Night   192
Abiku   193

Two poems from *A Shuttle in the Crypt* (1972):

Ujamaa   194
Bearings III: Amber Wall   194

NIGERIA
continued

John Pepper Clark (b.1935)

Seven poems from
A Reed in the Tide (1965):

Olokun	195
Night Rain	196
For Granny (from Hospital)	197
Cry of Birth	198
Abiku	199
A Child Asleep	200
The Leader	201

From *Casualties* (1970):

Season of Omens	201

Frank Aig-Imoukhuede (b.1935)

One Wife for One Man	203

Okogbule Wonodi (b.1936)

Planting	204
Salute to Icheke	205

Michael Echeruo (b.1937)

Melting Pot	206
Man and God Distinguished	207

Pol N Ndu (1940–78)

udude (at cock crow)	208
Evacuation	209

Onwuchekwa Jemie (b.1940)

Iroko   210
Toward a Poetics: 1 and 2   211

Aig Higo (b.1942)

Ritual Murder   213
Hidesong   213

Molara Ogundipe-Leslie (b.194?)

Song at the African Middle Class   214

Niyi Osundare (b.1947)

The Sand Seer   215
I Sing of Change   216

Odia Ofeimun (b.1950)

Let Them Choose Paths   217
A Naming Day   218
A Gong   219

Funso Aiyejina (b.1950)

Let Us Remember   220
May Ours Not Be   221

SAN TOMÉ   *Aldo do Espirito Santo* (b.1926)

Where Are the Men Seized in   225
this Wind of Madness?

SENEGAL   *Léopold Sédar Senghor* (b.1906)

In Memoriam   229
Night of Sine   230

SENEGAL *continued*	Luxembourg 1939	231
	Blues	232
	Prayer to Masks	233
	Visit	234
	What Dark Tempestuous Night	234
	New York	235
	You Held the Black Face	237
	I Will Pronounce Your Name	238
	Be Not Amazed	238

Birago Diop (b.1906)

	Diptych	239
	Vanity	240
	Ball	241
	Viaticum	241

David Diop (1927–60)

	Listen Comrades	243
	Your Presence	244
	The Renegade	244
	Africa	245
	The Vultures	246

SIERRA LEONE	*Syl Cheney-Coker* (b.1945)	

Six poems from *The Graveyard also has Teeth* (1980):

	On Being a Poet in Sierra Leone	249
	Poem for a Guerrilla Leader	250
	The Hunger of the Suffering Man	251
	Poem for a Lost Lover	252
	Letter to a Tormented Playwright	253
	The Road to Exile Thinking of Vallejo	254

From *The Blood in the Desert's Eyes*:

The Philosopher   256

SOUTH AFRICA   *Dennis Brutus* (b.1924)

At a Funeral   259
Nightsong: City   259
This Sun on this Rubble   260
Poems About Prison: I   260

Mazisi Kunene (b.1932)

The Echoes   262
Elegy   263
Thought on June 26   264

Sipho Sepamla (b.1932)

On Judgement Day   265
Civilization Aha   266
Talk to the Peach Tree   266

Keorapetse Kgositsile (b.1938)

The Air I Hear   267
Song for Ilva Mackay and
Mongane   268
The Present is a Dangerous Place
to Live: I and IV   269

Oswald Mtshali (b.1940)

Inside My Zulu Hut   271
Ride upon the Death Chariot   272
The Birth of Shaka   273

SOUTH AFRICA   *Arthur Nortje* (1942–70)
continued

    Up Late   274
    At Rest from the Grim Place   275

    Mongane Wally Serote (b.1944)

    The Growing   277
    Hell, Well, Heaven   277
    Ofay-Watcher Looks Back   279

UGANDA   *Okot p'Bitek* (1931–82)

    From The *Song of Lawino* (1966)   283

    From *Song of Prisoner* (1970)   285

ZAÏRE   *Antoine-Roger Bolamba* (b.1913)

    Portrait   289
    A Fistful of News   290

    Mukula Kadima-Nzuji (b.1947)

    Incantations of the Sea: Moando
    Coast   291
    Love in the Plural   291

    Notes on the Authors   293

    Sources of the Poems   304

    Index of First Lines   308

    Acknowledgements   314

Introduction

The Mozambiquan poet Noémia de Sousa writes ironically of a fellow countryman reduced to helotry in the mines of the Rand:

> And, stunned,
> Magaica lit a lamp
> to search for his lost illusions,
> for his youth and his health which stay buried
> deep in the mines of Johannesburg.
> Youth and health,
> the lost illusions
> which will shine like stars
> on some Lady's neck in some City's night.

Magaica's losses are sad enough; the helotry of the South African miner is lamented also in Felix Mnthali's poem for his father. Magaica lost his youth and health; thousands of his contemporaries lost their lives, or consumed many years of them away in the prison camps of Cape Verde, Rhodesia, South Africa and elsewhere. Loss of liberty, of life, of the hopes and companions of one's youth, runs through the poetry of this selection like a flood. The years during which most of it was written correspond with the anti-colonial wars which began in Madagascar in 1947 and continue to this day in Southern Africa. The same decades have seen civil war in Nigeria and Angola; the rise of many brutal dictatorships, some still flourishing; the imprisonment of many of Africa's most passionate and eloquent writers. How then can the note of loss not predominate, where so much has been lost? And yet it is strongly challenged here by other assertions: of love, aspiration, anger, hope and rediscovery. The effect, we believe, of reading these poems cannot be one of unmixed sadness or despair. There is still, in the continent and its poetry, a sense of youth, of new beginnings and untried possibilities, even while there is an equal insistence upon continuity and tradition, upon what is immemorial in the African experience and has survived all the ravages of recent centuries. The poets here collected obviously feel that it is their task not only to lament tragic and often irrecoverable loss, but to identify the points of growth and renewal in their world.

In the poetry of Angola, with which the selection opens, we find in equal measure anger and grief for all the comrades who fell and are still falling, the promise of triumphant return from 'the land of exile and silence' (Jofre Rocha), and the determination to fulfil the hopes which have sustained an armed struggle already more than twenty years old. Costa Andrade's *Fourth Poem of a Canto of Accusation* refers to the first and perhaps most pitiful losses of that struggle, the 50,000 slain indiscriminately after the attack on the Luanda prisons in February 1961. Angola's revolutionary anger is matched by that of the new Black South African poetry, running from Mazisi Kunene's *Thought on June 26* through Mtshali, Sepamla and Wally Serote. Its grief is echoed from San Tomé and Mozambique; anticipated in the powerful anti-colonial poetry of David Diop, already thirty years old; given an ironical twist in Okot p'Bitek's *Song of Prisoner* or a historical perspective of three centuries in the Congolese poets Tati-Loutard and U Tam'si. On almost every page here the cost is counted of what Africa has suffered, so that its fruit may 'gradually acquire/The bitter taste of liberty' (Diop). But Africa does not wish to appear always and only as the victim of its own tragedy. The passionate love poems of Mbella Sonne Dipoko or Syl Cheney-Coker, poems of filial piety, friendship, ironic mockery of pretension, funeral dirges, laments both of exile and of return, can all be found in these pages. The harvest is rich, despite a penalty which would discourage many from writing at all – the penalty of creating in a language not one's own or that of one's people.

A few poets here, important in their influence if not their numbers, have written extensively in their mother tongues and then translated their own work into English. The Ewe dirges of Kofi Awoonor, the Zulu poems of Mazisi Kunene and the energetic Luo songs of Okot p'Bitek are all examples of this indirect and often fruitful approach to the task of finding an acceptable English 'voice'.

The situation has been rather different where French and Portuguese are concerned. French was the language not only of *assimilation* but of the counter-assertion of *négritude*; hence poets in Senegal, Benin or Cameroun do not seem to have felt any compulsion to abandon it. Rather, they sought to turn it against their conquerors. Likewise in Angola, the movement of cultural and political resistance, *Let us Discover Angola*, which began in the late 1940s, involved many white and mulatto writers and artists as well as many black Africans. So, later, did the political and military cadres of the M.P.L.A. The language seemed to be that which could unite them, which could counter point for point the bland assertions of Portuguese imperial policy.

Except in South Africa, it would be hard to find elsewhere in the continent so many writers not themselves black who have suffered exile and imprisonment alongside their brothers as in Angola. Poetry and resistance went hand in hand, many poets becoming fighters and many fighters turning to poetry. Sung around the campfires of the guerrillas, these poems overcame all the barriers imposed by the illiteracy of the masses and the attempts of the colonial system to isolate them from the elites, the *'assimilados'*.

Anglophone poets in Africa have always been more ambivalent in their attitude towards a language which *has* acquired a life and flavour of its own in Africa, but which is still perceived by many as a colonial imposition which must sooner or later be rejected. It may be no coincidence, therefore, that the poets already mentioned who initially create their works in an African language and then translate them are all from the Anglophone areas of Africa. Here too we find poets writing in Pidgin (Aig-Imoukhuede) or trying to represent verbally some of the effects of drum poetry or flute poetry, as Okigbo did in *Lament of the Drums* and *Elegy for Alto*. The passage quoted from Okot's *Song of Prisoner* also seems to invoke the stamping of hundreds of feet which accompanies an Acoli funeral ceremony.

In comparison with these attempts to extend poetry in English back towards an indigenous poetic tradition, the work appearing in French and Portuguese may seem, in one sense, somewhat literary; somewhat addicted to purity of diction in what is, after all, a foreign language. Against that, however, it might be argued that the poetry of David Diop, the late Augustinho Neto or Jorge Rebelo, to name a few examples, has more revolutionary urgency, more grasp of immediate political reality, than we commonly encounter, South Africa apart, among the Anglophones.

This selection offers over two hundred poems, chosen from sixty-seven poets and twenty-three countries. The omission of a country must not be interpreted as an assertion that it has no poets. There are limits to editorial zeal as well as, no doubt, to editorial judgement. Perhaps we have missed work which would have been included if it had come before us. But we have not felt obliged to include a country for the sake of doing so. Nor have we included poems written in African languages and translated by another hand. Without an intimate knowledge of the original language, it would be impossible to judge the quality either of the original poem or of the translation; something which is possible when the poet himself brings his work before us. An anthology of poetry in African languages, valuable as it would be, requires the

21

collaboration of a whole team of editors who between them have a comprehensive knowledge of all the languages and poetic traditions of the continent. We have preferred to leave such a task to such a team, in the belief that what is included here has a value, a thrust and a shape of its own. The languages implanted by colonialism continue to carry, for better or for worse, a great part of Africa's creative expression.

What does this anthology tell us about the present state of the art in Africa? One may note that the countries which figured strongly in the first anthology, *Modern Poetry from Africa*, published over twenty years ago, have continued to do so. Senegal has perhaps lost some ground, compared with its eminence in the 1940s and 1950s. South Africa has moved into the forefront, after being relatively poor in black Anglophone poets until recent years. Nigeria continues prolific in poets, but it does after all contain almost half the continent's black population, and some degree of domination is to be expected. By placing poets in order of their dates of birth we hope to show the emergence of a modern poetic tradition, where it exists. The poets anthologized from South Africa, Angola and Nigeria, for example, represent in poetic terms at least three distinct generations.

Most of the major poets anthologized before have continued active and examples of their recent work have been included here. Some important new talents are here represented for the first time: these include Syl Cheney-Coker of Sierra Leone, Ahmed Tidjani-Cissé of Guinea, Kofi Anyidoho of Ghana, Mukula Kadima-Nzuji of Zaïre, Jack Mapenje of Malawi and Jared Angira of Kenya, as well as many new poets from South Africa, Angola and other former Portuguese lands. These new writers have extended the range of African poetry in many directions; whether in the passionate grief of Costa Andrade; the sophisticated irony of Tidjani-Cissé, Sepamla and Mapenje; the philosophical curiosity of Angira; or the musings of Cheney-Coker on the destiny of the poet. Africa's turbulent and often tragic progress through the twentieth century has not passed unchronicled by its poets The greater critical attention given to fiction in recent decades is more a reflection upon the critics than upon the continued vigour and invention of the poetry.

Lastly, something should be said about the concept of the modern in African poetry. In a recent essay, Lewis Nkosi has written interestingly on this topic, and specifically on many of the poets included here. His conclusions are very close to those which have guided us in excluding the 'Pioneer Poets' of Anglophone Africa (Dei-Anang, Armattoe,

Osadebey, Vilakazi, Dhlomo, etc.), whilst including many Francophone poets of the same generation. Nkosi writes:

> Under the heading of 'the moderns' we shall, therefore, be discussing a variety of African poets, with a heterogeneity of styles and techniques; in the end what seems to unite them, and equally what seems to separate them from 'the pioneer poets', is a fundamental pre-occupation with technique as important both in itself as well as providing the essential means for expressing a radically transformed cultural and political situation ... In contrast, what seems to have absorbed all the energies of 'the pioneer poets' were certain themes they regarded as urgent, method was left to look after itself ... lack of a fresh and original approach made the verse seem dull and uninspired.*

A major concern with craft is inseparable from real achievement in poetry. A poet writing in a European language, even if he wishes to make a counter-statement against the nation which brought it, must at least be aware of the current state of poetic form and diction in that language. The African *négritude* poets displayed such an awareness of the state of French poetry (including that of such black poets as Damas and Césaire), as well as being much more aware of Langston Hughes and the Harlem poets than their Anglophone contemporaries were. Hence they were able to find an authentic voice for their poetry. Even if the polarities on which it was built – African innocence vs white depravity/ black emotion vs white intellect/a decadent Europe vs an unchanging idyllic Africa – now look somewhat simplistic and inadequate, the poetry often transcends them, as in the best work of Senghor and the Diops. And it transcends them partly because of its concern with craft and its awareness of what is happening in the same language elsewhere in the world. By contrast, the Pioneers seem not only parochial but strangely archaic, with stanzas and diction derived from hymns or Victorian ballads. Only with the generation of Okara, soon followed by Okigbo, Soyinka, Clark and others, do we get poets who show this awareness of the state of the art and the English language in their time. Even the poets working closest to a particular vernacular tradition, like Okot, Awoonor and Kunene, show this same awareness. Even if the poetry of the early 1960s in Ibadan often suffers from an overdose of Pound, Hopkins or Eliot, the better poets soon transcended that phase and found a poetic style which was both African and contemporary. The development shown by Okigbo in the five years between 1961 and

---

*Lewis Nkosi, 'Modern African Poetry: its Themes and Styles, in *Tasks and Masks* (Longmans, 1981), pp. 126–7.

1966 would have been unthinkable without his intense interest in formal experiment and his respect for good poetry appearing elsewhere. He must, for example, have been the first Nigerian poet to read the Beat Poets, who were discovering a new audience for poetry in America in those same years.

So far as Lusophone poetry is concerned, the forcing house seems to have been the desire to use poetry to voice the suffering of the anonymous masses, not just that of the poet. The result was the simple, muscular and direct poetry of Neto, Jacinto, Rebelo, Andrade and others; a poetry easily adapted to the demands of nations literally fighting for their liberty. This was a poetry which could not fail to be contemporary, in its language as well as its concerns, if it was to speak to the guerrillas and be wielded by them.

Without searching for any phoney universalism, it must be recognized that there is an international dimension to the art of poetry in the modern world. How else can we explain why the Nicaraguan Rubén Dario revivified the poetry of Spain itself in the late nineteenth century, or the complete reshaping of English poetry achieved by Pound, Eliot and Yeats, none of them English? A literal translation of lines from an African original, though often felicitous and strong, sometimes fails to ring in English. This happens occasionally in Awoonor's early work, and more often in Kunene's, because the idiom of the Zulu praise-poem does not always sit easily in the new language. And it is the language in which the poetry comes to us which will determine our judgement of the poem. It looks as if the forging of an authentic style, whether in English, French or Portuguese, cannot be done in the sort of nationalistic isolation apparently prescribed by some critics.* The poet will be no less African for being also a part of the confraternity of poets handling the same language in the same time.

*See, for example, the chapter on 'African Poetry and its Critics', in *Toward the Decolonization of African Literature*, by Chinweizu, Onwuchekwa Jemie and Ihechukwu Madubuike (Enugu, Fourth Dimension Publishers, 1980).

Angola

Augustinho Neto

Farewell at the Moment of Parting

My mother
(oh black mothers whose children have departed)
you taught me to wait and to hope
as you have done through the disastrous hours

But in me
life has killed that mysterious hope

I wait no more
it is I who am awaited

Hope is ourselves
your children
travelling towards a faith that feeds life

We the naked children of the bush sanzalas
unschooled urchins who play with balls of rags
on the noonday plains
ourselves
hired to burn out our lives in coffee fields
ignorant black men
who must respect the whites
and fear the rich
we are your children of the native quarters
which the electricity never reaches
men dying drunk
abandoned to the rhythm of death's tom-toms
your children
who hunger
who thirst
who are ashamed to call you mother
who are afraid to cross the streets
who are afraid of men

It is ourselves
the hope of life recovered.

African Poem

There on the horizon
the fire
and the dark silhouettes of the imbondeiro trees
with their arms raised
in the air the green smell of burnt palm trees

On the road
the line of Bailundo porters
groaning under their loads of crueira*

in the room
the sweet sweet-eyed mulatress
retouching her face with rouge and rice-powder
the woman under her many clothes moving her hips
on the bed
the sleepless man thinking
of buying knives and forks to eat with at a table

On the sky the reflections
of the fire
and the silhouette of the blacks at the drums
with their arms raised
in the air the warm tune of marimbas

On the road the porters
in the room the mulatress
on the bed the sleepless man

The burning coals consuming
consuming with fire
the warm country of the horizons.

*Crueira = maize flour.

Kinaxixi

I was glad to sit down
on a bench in Kinaxixi
at six o'clock of a hot evening
and just sit there . . .

Someone would come
maybe
to sit beside me

And I would see the black faces
of the people going uptown
in no hurry
expressing absence in the
jumbled Kimbundu they conversed in.

I would see the tired footsteps
of the servants whose fathers also were servants
looking for love here, glory there, wanting
something more than drunkenness in every
alcohol.

Neither happiness nor hate.

After the sun had set
lights would be turned on and I
would wander off
thinking that our life after all is simple
too simple
for anyone who is tired and still has to walk.

The Grieved Lands

The grieved lands of Africa
in the tearful woes of ancient and modern slave
in the degrading sweat of impure dance
of other seas
grieved

The grieved lands of Africa
in the infamous sensation of the stunning perfume of the
flower
crushed in the forest

by the wickedness of iron and fire
the grieved lands

The grieved lands of Africa
in the dream soon undone in jinglings of gaolers' keys
and in the stifled laughter and victorious voice of laments
and in the unconscious brilliance of hidden sensations
of the grieved lands of Africa

                Alive
                in themselves and with us alive

They bubble up in dreams
decked with dances by baobabs over balances
by the antelope
in the perpetual alliance of everything that lives

They shout out the sound of life
shout it
even the corpses thrown up by the Atlantic
in putrid offering of incoherence and death
and in the clearness of rivers

They live
the grieved lands of Africa
in the harmonious sound of consciences
contained in the honest blood of men
in the strong desire of men
in the sincerity of men
in the pure and simple rightness of the stars' existence

They live
the grieved lands of Africa
because we are living
and are imperishable particles
of the grieved lands of Africa.

Antonio Jacinto

Monangamba

On that big estate there is no rain
it's the sweat of my brow that waters the crops:

On that big estate there is coffee ripe
and that cherry-redness
is drops of my blood turned sap.

> The coffee will be roasted,
> ground, and crushed,
> will turn black, black with the colour of the *contratado*.*

Black with the colour of the *contratado*!

Ask the birds that sing,
the streams in carefree wandering
and the high wind from inland:

> Who gets up early? Who goes to toil?
> Who is it carries on the long road
> the hammock or bunch of kernels?
> Who reaps and for pay gets scorn
> rotten maize, rotten fish,
> ragged clothes, fifty *angolares*†
> beating for biting back?

Who?

> Who makes the millet grow
>
> and the orange groves to flower?
> – Who?

Who gives the money for the boss to buy
cars, machinery, women
　and Negro heads for motors?

contratado = contract labourer.　　†*angolares* = unit of money.

Who makes the white man prosper,
grow big-bellied – get much money?
– Who?

And the birds that sing,
the streams in carefree wandering
and the high wind from inland
will answer:

– Monangambeeee....

Ah! Let me at least climb the palm trees
Let me drink wine, palm wine
and fuddled by my drunkness forget

– Monangambeee....

Poem of Alienation

This is not yet my poem
the poem of my soul and of my blood
no
I still lack knowledge and power to write my poem
the great poem I feel already turning in me

My poem wanders aimlessly
in the bush or in the city
in the voice of the wind
in the surge of the sea
in the Aspect and the Being

My poem steps outside
wrapped in showy cloths
selling itself
selling
   '*lemons, buy my le-e-e-emons*'

My poem runs through the streets
with a putrid cloth pad on its head
offering itself
offering
   '*mackerel, sardine, sprats
   fine fish, fine fi-i-i-sh . . .*'

My poem trudges the streets
'here J'urnal' 'Dai-i-i-ly'
and no newspaper yet carries my poem

My poem goes into the cafés
'lott'ry draw-a tomorra lott'ry draw-a tomorra'
and the draw of my poem
wheel as it wheels
whirl as it whirls
never changes
   'lott'ry draw-a tomorra
   lott'ry draw-a tomorra'

My poem comes from the township
on Saturdays bring the washing
on Mondays take the washing
on Saturdays surrender the washing and surrender self
on Mondays surrender self and take the washing

My poem is in the suffering
of the laundress's daughter
shyly
in the closed room
of a worthless boss idling
to build up an appetite for the violation

My poem is the prostitute
in the township at the broken door of her hut
   'hurry hurry
   pay your money
   come and sleep with me'

My poem lightheartedly plays at ball
in a crowd where everyone is a servant
and shouts
   'offside goal goal'

My poem is a contract worker
goes to the coffee fields to work
the contract is a burden
that is hard to load
   'contract wor-r-r-ker'

My poem walks barefoot in the street

My poem loads sacks in the port
fills holds
empties holds
and finds strength in singing
   'tué tué tué trr
   arrimbuim puim puim'

My poem goes tied in ropes
met a policeman
paid a fine, the boss
forgot to sign the pass
goes on the roadwork
with hair shorn
   'head shaved
   chicken braised
   o Zé'

a goad that weighs
a whip that plays

My poem goes to market works in the kitchen
goes to the workbench
fills the tavern and the gaol
is poor ragged and dirty
lives in benighted ignorance
my poem knows nothing of itself
nor how to plead

My poem was made to give itself
to surrender itself
without asking for anything

But my poem is not fatalist
my poem is a poem that already wants
and already knows
my poem is I-white
mounted on me-black
riding through life.

Letter from a Contract Worker

I wanted to write you a letter
my love,
a letter that would tell
of this desire
to see you
of this fear
of losing you
of this more than benevolence that I feel
of this indefinable ill that pursues me
of this yearning to which I live in total surrender . . .

I wanted to write you a letter
my love,
a letter of intimate secrets,
a letter of memories of you,
of you
of your lips red as henna
of your hair black as mud
of your eyes sweet as honey
of your breasts hard as wild orange
of your lynx gait
and of your caresses
such that I can find no better here . . .
I wanted to write you a letter
my love,
that would recall the days in our haunts
our nights lost in the long grass
that would recall the shade falling on us from the plum
trees
the moon filtering through the endless palm trees
that would recall the madness
of our passion
and the bitterness
of our separation . . .

I wanted to write you a letter
my love,
that you would not read without sighing
that you would hide from papa Bombo
that you would withhold from mama Kieza

that you would reread without the coldness
of forgetting
a letter to which in all Kilombo
no other would stand comparison . . .

I wanted to write you a letter
my love
a letter that would be brought to you by the passing wind
a letter that the cashews and coffee trees
the hyenas and buffaloes
the alligators and grayling
could understand
so that if the wind should lose it on the way
the beasts and plants
with pity for our sharp suffering
from song to song
lament to lament
gabble to gabble
would bring you pure and hot
the burning words
the sorrowful words of the letter
I wanted to write to you my love . . .

I wanted to write you a letter . . .

But oh my love, I cannot understand
why it is, why it is, why it is, my dear
that you cannot read
and I – Oh the hopelessness! – cannot write!

Costa Andrade

Fourth Poem of a Canto of Accusation

There are on the earth 50,000 dead whom no one mourned
   on the earth
     unburied
       50,000 dead

whom no one mourned.

A thousand Guernicas and the message in the brushes of
Orozco and of Siqueiros
as broad as the sea this silence
spread across the land

     as if the rains had rained blood
     as if the rough hair were grass for many yards
     as if the mouths condemned
     at the very instant of their 50,000 deaths
     all the living of the earth.

There are on the earth 50,000 dead
whom no one mourned

no one . . .

The Mothers of Angola
   have fallen with their sons.

Ngudia Wendel

We Shall Return, Luanda

Luanda, you are like a white seagull
on the ocean crest –
bright streets under the white sun,
flight of green palm trees . . .
but we have seen you grow black, Luanda,
since the bitter fourth of February
when the blood of combatants for liberty
was spilled in your streets –
in your bright streets,
Mother Luanda.

We remember that day
your streets seething with crowds
like the Cuanza in flood.
Our rage thundered louder than the cannon
in the executioner's fortress.

And we went to the attack through a hail of lead
and we died in your streets –
in your bright streets,
Mother Luanda.

Through battle we won victory
on that bitter day,
hundreds of our black brothers
were stretched out for eternity in your streets.

We came through the bush
through the long tropical rains,
the wounded moaned on their stretchers
ammunition belts stained their backs,
legs were caught fast in treacherous swamps,
but we came on to see you,
our Mother Luanda.

But you stranger and hangman
have drowned Luanda in blood,
you have fed on the living body for ages
like the bush tick.
Now you tremble and cling to your sandbags
and steel helmets
and the shelter of machine guns
wisely, for you know
that the moment of reckoning
is nigh.

One day we shall come out of the bush
through the smoke of the last explosives
and we shall see you, Luanda,
the ships in the bay –
big-bellied ships, hurriedly packed
with the last of the murderers ...
That day is not over the hills, far away,
it is close at hand
our black brothers give their lives for it.
We shall return, Mother Luanda!

Jofre Rocha

Poem of Return

When I return from the land of exile and silence,
do not bring me flowers.

Bring me rather all the dews,
tears of dawns which witnessed dramas.
Bring me the immense hunger for love
and the plaint of tumid sexes in star-studded night.
Bring me the long night of sleeplessness
with mothers mourning, their arms bereft of sons.

When I return from the land of exile and silence,
no, do not bring me flowers . . .

Bring me only, just this
the last wish of heroes fallen at day-break
with a wingless stone in hand
and a thread of anger snaking from their eyes.

Ruy Duarte de Carvalho

I Come from a South

I came to the east
to gauge the dimension of night
in broad gestures
that I devised in the south
watching flocks and plains
bright
like thighs remembered in May.

I come from a south
measured clearly
in transparency of tomorrow's fresh water.
From a circular time
free of seasons.
From a nation of transhumant bodies
blurred
in the colour of the thorned crust
of a black ground chased in live coal.

Benin (Dahomey)

Emile Ologoudou

Vespers

Autumnal skies
the sun has smashed his jar of red oil,
on this day of great anger over the earth
I will leave the dainty lettering of the sky
with
this
message heavy as a bobbin of lead
to tell my people what I am told to tell them,
it is the fixed invective of the other shore
and
the heart at this work for the rest of my life,
I shall see no more this sun which totters,
this light which crumples under the slow shadows,
ah!
what are they these things which capsize
in
the sea of my being at the hour of departure?
it is, at the very summit of the soul,
terror before the thousand promises we shall be able to keep.

Liberty

The white carcases
of
ships
sought desperately
the visible island with its golden mist,
the native isle of insurrection,
stage at evening of the most tragic adventures,
we were tossed
on the waves of the same sorrow,
and discord
had not yet blown towards us the sands
of
its evidence,
exuberance still reigned over the happy bay,
that day when we made long funerals
for all the things
we had to bury . . .

Cameroun

Simon Mpondo

The signs of the rains say-o
Say maybe what everyone wants to hear
Soon there will be plenty of water
Plenty of summer and mud
That's the message we read in the sight
Of the season of rains

The Season of the Rains

The season of the rains
Signs its name in a thousand fashions
Those who want to read omens there
Will find their signs
In the flowering beard of the maize
And in the black or red rings of millipedes
Does the swallow's departure for the Margui-Wandala
Announce many storms and floods along the Wouri?
Has the spider woven its web
Stored up insects and light and the sun's warmth
To vanquish a cold season of a thousand days?
Does the plucked chicken speak of hard or easy times?

What says the black millipede?
What says the red millipede?
They say what the omens say
Yes or no or even perhaps
These are the signs
But they tell mainly what happened in the dry season
And not what the rains will bring forth
Plenty of labour in the dry days
Translates itself as maize in the wet
And in food for millipedes red or black
But the millipede's colour
And the largeness of its rings
Which the sorcerer measures in his secret hut
Owe nothing to the season
Those colours will always vary
Some rings will always be large
And some narrow
Let each person make of it what he will

CAMEROUN

The signs of the rainy season
Say exactly what everyone wants to hear
Surely there will be plenty of water
Plenty of swamps and mud
That's the message we read in the signs
Of the season of rains.

Mbella Sonne Dipoko

Our Life

An ailing bird over the desert made its agony
A song blown through the air
As at the oasis
Drawers of water said
How low it flies oh how touching its song

The winged hope that proved to be a dream
(Masked our destiny with a black hood)

As in the cities we said the same prayers
As in the villages we espoused ancestral myths
Transmitting our frustration our life our mortality
To the young country of tomorrow and day after tomorrow
Flattering ourselves with the charity of the blood-donor's love.

Pain

All was quiet in this park
Until the wind, like a gasping messenger, announced
The tyrant's coming
Then did the branches talk in agony.
You remember that raging storm?

In their fear despairing flowers nevertheless held
Bouquets to the grim king;
Meteors were the tassels of his crown
While like branches that only spoke when the storm menaced
We cried in agony as we fell
Slashed by the cold blade of an invisible sword.

Mutilated, our limbs were swept away by the rain;
But not our blood;
Indelible, it stuck on the walls
Like wild gum on tree-trunks.

Exile

In silence
The overloaded canoe leaves our shores

But who are these soldiers in camouflage,
These clouds going to rain in foreign lands?

The night is losing its treasures
The future seems a myth
Warped on a loom worked by lazy hands.

But perhaps all is not without some good for us
As from the door of a shack a thousand miles away
The scaly hand of a child takes in greeting
The long and skinny fingers of the rain.

A Poem of Villeneuve St Georges
(for M – C)

I am tempted to think of you
Now that I have grown old
And date my sadness
To the madness of your love.

All those flowers you hung
On my gate
All those flowers the wind blew
On the snow!
Why must I remember them now
And recall you calling me
Like a screech-owl
While I watched you
Through the window-pane
And the moon was over the Seine
And Africa was far away
And you were calling
And then crying
In the snow of exile
And the neighbour's dog barking as if bored
By the excesses of your tenderness?

When I came down for you
And opened the gate
Cursing the cold of your land
You always went and stood
Under the poplars of the river Yerres
At the bottom of the garden
Silently watching its Seine-bound waters;
And the moon might take to the clouds
Casting a vast shadow
That sometimes seemed to reach our hearts.

And then following me upstairs
You stopped a while on the balcony
As high as which the vines of the garden grew
With those grapes which had survived
The end of the summer
You picked a few grapes
Which we ate.
I remember their taste
Which was that of our kisses.

And then in the room
You in such a hurry to undress
And you always brought
A white and a black candle which you lit.
Their flames were the same colour
Of the fire glowing in the grate
And you were no longer white
You were brown
By the light of the fires of love
At midnight
Years ago.

From My Parisian Diary

Thirty centimes is all the money I have left
But I am full of hope without knowing why.
I laugh at the world and laugh at myself
Something of a child at thirty-five.
It has been a hard life since I ran out of cynicism
And stopped selling for a commission
Just any newspaper in the world
Deciding exclusively on pamphlets of the Left
By which I am now earning death by instalment
On a starvation diet
And the rent is long overdue.
Surely this is not a way of earning a living
Peddling slogans of a better world
In the garrison of troops armed to defend these cruel days.
But the struggle must continue
And we must open new fronts even in our dreams.

Patrice Kayo

Song of the Initiate

All the wives of my father
      pulled my mother to bits
But their children cannot dance
It is I who have taken my father's stool
And my mother has become queen
All the wives of my father my wives
      and servants of my mother.

The mother of those who cannot dance
      has never borne children
Her children are nothing but epileptics
      The initiate alone with the chief.

If only I were a river!
I would roll down all silvery
And in the compound of the non-initiate
      I would become a swamp.

I am only a dealer in pigs
      and in chickens
But if you have any pearls or little bells
      I will buy them.
The only son alone
Is sure of his father's stool.
The panther's child does not fear the night
I can dance all the dances
And my mother eats nothing but the flesh of sparrowhawks.

War

Thunderous vapours!
water-spout with lion's teeth

A trumpet sounds the end of things
with its scabby tongue

But no, but no
The forests and mountains are still calving
and in his velvety pot
God sleeps on his anvil

Tossing fate to the winds
gun at the ready
the Orphan man goes forth
with his thoughts on his nose

At the market where one grinds one's teeth
stamp
lacerate yourself
We have ground our teeth
stamped
and lacerated ourselves
And it was our destiny.

For the altar of expiation
we would be the incense
and awaken God from his coma
Let him abolish us
And begin his creation afresh
Let him shatter science
extinguish the embers
And plunge us again in the sweetness
of innocent day.

For man if you pass
from God's vassal to his equal
and if upon the scaffold
You decapitate death
the new God
You would still be no less monstrous.

Cape Verde Islands

Onésima Silveira

A Different Poem

The people of the islands want a different poem
For the people of the islands;
A poem without exiles complaining
In the calm of their existence;
A poem without children nourished
On the black milk of aborted time
A poem without mothers gazing
At the vision of their sons, motherless.
The people of the islands want a different poem
For the people of the islands:
A poem without arms in need of work
Nor mouths in need of bread
A poem without boats ballasted with people
On the road to the South
A poem without words choked
By the harrows of silence.
The people of the islands want a different poem
For the people of the islands:
A poem with sap rising in the heart of the BEGINNING
A poem with Batuque and tchabeta and the badias of St Catherine,
A poem with shaking hips and laughing ivory.
The people of the islands want a different poem
For the people of the islands:
A poem without men who lose the seas' grace
and the fantasy of the main compass points.

Congo Republic

Tchicaya U Tam'si

Three poems from *Feu de Brousse* (1957)

Brush-fire

The fire the river that's to say
the sea to drink following the sand
the feet the hands
within the heart to love
this river that lives in me repeoples me
only to you I said around the fire

my race
it flows here and there a river
the flames are the looks
of those who brood upon it
I said to you
my race
remembers
the taste of bronze drunk hot.

Dance to the Amulets

Come over here
our grass is rich
come you fawns

gestures and stabs of sickly hands
curving then unripping of conception
one – who? – you shape my fate
come you fawns

over here the suppleness of mornings
and the blood masked here
and the rainbow-coloured dream the rope at the neck
come over here

our grass is rich here
my first coming
was the harsh explosion of a flint
solitude
my mother promised me to light.

A Mat to Weave

he came to deliver the secret of the sun
and wanted to write the poem of his life

why crystals in his blood
why globules in his laughter

his soul was ready
when someone called him
dirty wog

still he is left with the gentle arch of his laughter
and the giant tree with a living cleft
what was that country where he lived a beast
behind the beasts before behind the beasts

his stream was the safest of cups
because it was of bronze
because it was his living flesh

it was then that he said to himself
no my life is not a poem

here is the tree here is the water here are the stones
and then the priest of the future

it is better to love wine
and rise in the morning
he was advised

but no more birds within the tenderness of mothers
dirty wog
he is the younger brother to fire

the bush begins here
and the sea is no more than the memory of gulls
all standing upright tooth-to-tooth
against the spume of a deadly dance

the tree was the leafiest
the bark of the tree was the tenderest
after the forest was burnt what more to say

why was there absinthe in the wine
why restore in the hearts
the crocodiles the canoers
and the wave of the stream
the grains of sand between the teeth
is it thus that one breaks the world
no
no
his stream was the gentlest of cups
the safest
it was his most living flesh

here begins the poem of his life
he was trained in a school
he was trained in a studio
and he saw roads planted with sphinxes

still he is left with the soft arch of his laughter
then the tree then the water then the leaves

that is why you will see him
the marching canoers have raised once more
against the haulers of french cotton
their cries
this flight is a flight of doves

the leeches did not know the bitterness
of this blood
in the purest of cups

dirty gollywog
behold my congolese head

it is the purest of cups.

Four poems from *Epitomé* (1962)

A bouquet of faded flowers in my letterbox . . .

I was naked for the first kiss of my mother
I was naked before Sammy and before men

I would be cold already
without this taste of black salt
in your black blood

I have the claws of a woman in my flesh
I bleed for her delight in love
But hide from me the image of her god
that fakir whose grin desalts my soul
and let the ferns
hold in the earth
the freshness of a patch of violent water.

These flowers in my letterbox, I cross my fingers to caress them and the con-
science of the world is silent with me over the drama of Léopoldville – I spit
into the Seine like all good poets.

What do I want with a thousand stars in broad daylight
the rapt surrealist
in one of them at midnight
has blessed my crazy reason

My reason is the memory of a levitation
it knits a blue stocking for the violated night
it kindles hell in the black flames it ends
the purification of my sinful swan
which once fixed a halo of pollen

on the head of a lustful black crab
my reason makes me difficult and faithless
in the abstract of my passion.

My prick is not even a root of the tree,
to speak as that tree rustles
would give a rustic perfume
to the game of my flight
and put less blood on the hands of my quest.

The disasters unfold in silence
as one loved them in childhood memory
and a grey rain serves all our dreams
forcing me to become a forger
and holy assassin
despite the equinox
despite myself
despite the sorcery of the smiles
of my obedient black brothers

And then
what would you have me say of this silence
squatting beside my own conscience?

They give you what they have eaten and what they have not known how to
keep. The shadow, like them, had a certain reticence.
I am full of spite with the sun.

You must be from my country
I see it by the tick
of your soul around the eyelashes
and besides you dance when you are sad
you must be from my country

Keep moving time is waiting to seduce us
learn from this that the oil in your lamp
is really my blood brimming up
and that, if it overflows, you mustn't light your lamp
we must have a dark corner somewhere
for our ancient orisons

All of us from the same umbilical cord
But who knows where we fetch
our awkward heads

Often the silences
reeking of iodine ravage us
with lecherous resolves
for my beardless conscience
ravage us alone.

The Scorner

I drink to your glory my god
You who have made me so sad
You have given me a people who are not distillers of gin

What wine shall I drink to your *jubilate*
In this country which has no vines
In this desert all the bushes are of cactus
Shall I take their crop of flowers
for flames of the burning bush of your desire
Tell me in what Egypt my people's feet lie chained

Christ I laugh at your sadness
O my sweet Christ
Thorn for thorn
We have a common crown of thorns
I will be converted because you tempt me
Joseph comes to me
I suck already the breast of the Virgin your mother
I count more than your one Judas on my fingers
My eyes lie to my soul
Where the world is a lamb your pascal lamb – Christ
I will waltz to the tune of your slow sadness.

Two poems from *Le Ventre* (1964)

1

'The Congo is myself' (Lumumba)

I myself will be the stage for my salvation!
Already velvet breaks the silences
with evanescent wings
which snow upon the oil-lamp.

Slobber within the masks will serve better for this carnival
than grinning on a thousand different notes,
But since I have only one face
Over that alone shall I pass my hand.
The flat horizon of this country splits my heart
If I recoil everything bristles suddenly!
I will stay at the gate with the wind in my side
but with tornadoes in my belly

2

I tear at my belly,
Neither seawrack nor iodine
nor the very algae have so much
tenderness in their caress
as my lips knew once
before the earth was insulted
by a galloping herd of ventriloquist jackals!

The belly
always with that sickening warmth
as of the charnel-house.

From *L'Arc Musical* (1970)

Epitaph

We are this union
of water salt and earth
of sunshine and flesh
bespattering the sun
no more among the sea marks
but because there is this song
which ruins all the gulfs
which recreates a genesis
of wind weather and flesh!

I predict a babel
of unoxidized steel
or of crossed blood
mixed in the dregs of all surges!
After the red man,
after the black man,
after the yellow man,
after the white man,
there is already the man of bronze
sole alloy of the soft fires
we have still to ford.

Jean-Baptiste Tati-Loutard

Four poems from *Poèmes de la Mer* (1968)

News of My Mother

I am now very high upon the tree of the seasons;
Far below I see the firm earth of the past.
When the fields opened themselves to the flow of seed
Before the baobab took aim at a flight of birds
With the first call of the sun,
It was your footsteps which sang around me:
A shower of bells chiming with my ablutions.
I am now very high upon the tree of the seasons.
Know by this fifteenth day of the moon
It is these tears – up till now –
Which fill your absence,
Which lighten drop by drop your image
Too heavy on my pupil;
Each night I waken drenched through with your pain
Even as if you lived in me again.

The Voices

Far across the waves, the wing of a gull
Ventilates a sea full of impurities –
The insult and darkness of refusal –
I remember it through the navel
Which ties me to the centuries of wrong.
The sea has assembled all their bones
Under the cross of the reefs;
They sleep their black oceanic slumber
In the heavy shroud of the silent deeps.
But I have an eye to pierce the darkness
Better than the fine fingers of sunlight
And an ear which hears the groans
Even the squalls cannot disperse,

An ear which catches the sound of a plunge
The stillest waters cannot cover.

Submarine Tombs

With my seven-fold inquisitorial eye,
More obscene than the urban wind,
I have raised up through its rippling folds
A dress of blue snake-skin
Horrible! All the side of a race
Lies there, spent,
Across the huge blocks of the generations.

Our liberty still weighs upon us
Seaweed and coral brothers
Who have never ceased to watch over our dead.
One day we will reward your constancy as it deserves,
And for their funerals we will dry up the sea.

Pilgrimage to Loango Strand

I have followed to this strand the scent of their blood
Of my blood
Forgetting other scars burnt by the hard wind
In days gone by; here I'll stop:
Life sickens me; I will go no further.
Even the path falters before the memory-post
Of an embarcation.
The sea still describes infinity
To this harbour, rocking its pendulum
Through three centuries;
And God's spirit still circles above the waters
Of this great flat silence
Pecked by the voyaging gulls.
I shall not continue my pilgrimage
Over the submarine roadway paved with bones
Until the distant resurgence of Jamestown
Amid the camps of death flowered with cotton.
Let noble Africa raise its own cenotaphs
For the repose of those heavy-hearted dead
Who went spilling their bitterness
Over the spume of the waves.

Two poems from *Les Racines Congolaises* (1968)

Noonday in Immaturity

With a dozen blows the clock betrays the pulse of time,
And the day-forged sun
Now begins its retreat amid a blaze of sparks.
The walls of races, of banks, of asylums
Blind me; I watch; far away
A single gap opens in the wall of fate,
Far off far off, it's the vast estuary of death
Where all my daily dreams converge.
As all the poems of my immaturity flare up
I will keep the ashes of their death on my face
Until the new germination.
I feel myself lonely and slender in the mirror of the lightning.

The tree my friend turns down his wick
Which watched over my thirst for the shadows;
I go forth in the sunlight
And, diviner with empty bag, I walk painfully
Through the fires of the centre.

Death and Rebirth

May the hide of the earth split beneath my feet,
May the valve of the sky open and show me
The high niche of the sun or the immense reach of the stars.
I shall fear nothing.

Does Death call me? Will it at least offer me
A mirror, a sheet of light where I can glimpse
My profile beyond the grave?

I am a seeding branch of this world,
My dreams flourish in the sunlight
Not in the gloomy swarming of the molluscs,
I balance myself in the wind;

I dizzy myself with all the gifts of day and night,
In passing I pluck the drunken birds from space: take them!
The serpent comes here each morning to my patch of dew

72

To lap at the source of his cry!
Like him, I throw myself ever higher and further,
No one sees how I prosper in the shadow of my secret;
I shall not respond to that call which rises from the thickets
Of the night.

Let the sea flow back upon itself with its cargo
Of salt and fishes! Let the sky split its azure lining!
Let the sun burst in a tourniquet of fire!
Why shouldn't it start with the elements?
I am at the dawn of a people beginning a long march:
I shall see them break from their coop in all the sweat
Of their souls, as the sun breaks from the channels of the East
In a great transpiration of Light!

Emmanuel Dongala

Fantasy under the Moon

(Blues for a muted trumpet)

I climbed towards you on a ray of moonlight
that filtered through a hole in my straw-thatched house
When I had reached the smiling arch of your mouth among the stars
you came to me
open under the sea of your body the heaving wave under my body
my heart beating to the rhythm of yours moving to the rhythm of your
    tribe the people of the mountain;
your serpent form writhing beneath mine
I sucked your cobra's poison from your broken lips
and my fever mounted like a sickness.

I visited last night our banana grove of the first time.
When I reached those great sombre aisles
under which we pressed each other behind your mother's back
under the teasing trumpet of thirsty mosquitoes
the circle of my arms about your shadow your phantom
all at once hung emptier than the rope of a wine-tapper
embracing the palm tree.

I don't know why that large cloud crossing the moon
suddenly made the tide of your body fall.
Like oiled wrestlers at a festival
who feel their adversary slide between their arms
powerless I felt you slip from mine
under the moon's light white as this wine as your teeth which made you
    so gay
as you fluttered wildly in the circle of the dance
while your mother warned you not to come near me.

I looked up at the sky from the depths of my hut;
the moon was only a smile, your white smile congealed.

74

Gambia

Lenrie Peters

Homecoming

The present reigned supreme
  Like the shallow floods over the gutters
Over the raw paths where we had been,
  The house with the shutters.

Too strange the sudden change
  Of the times we buried when we left
The times before we had properly arranged
  The memories that we kept.

Our sapless roots have fed
  The wind-swept seedlings of another age.
Luxuriant weeds have grown where we led
  The Virgins to the water's edge.

There at the edge of the town
  Just by the burial ground
Stands the house without a shadow
  Lived in by new skeletons.

That is all that is left
  To greet us on the home-coming
After we have paced the world
  And longed for returning.

Song

Clawed green-eyed
Feline of night
Palsy-breasted
Selling old boot
On wet pavement
In hour-glass baskets
Coconut bellied
Unyielding copra

Gland exhausted
Love fatigued
Worm-tunnelled sod
Prostituted fruit of Eve
Edging the Park trees
Like dancing Caterpillars
In folded leaves
Softened by Social Conscience
Hounded by Prudes
Friend of the falling star
Victim of the lonely bed.

We Have Come Home

We have come home
From the bloodless war
With sunken hearts
Our boots full of pride –
From the true massacre of the soul
When we have asked
'What does it cost
To be loved and left alone?'

We have come home,
Bringing the pledge
Which is written in rainbow colours
Across the sky – for burial
But it is not the time
To lay wreaths
For yesterday's crimes
Night threatens
Time dissolves
And there is no acquaintance
With tomorrow
The gurgling drums
Echo the star
The forest howls –
And between the trees
The dark sun appears.

We have come home
When the dawn falters
Singing songs of other lands
The Death March
Violating our ears
Knowing all our lore and tears
Determined by the spinning coin.

We have come home
To the green foothills
To drink from the cry
Of warm and mellow birdsong.
To the hot beaches
Where boats go out to sea
Threshing the ocean's harvest
And the harassing, plunging
gliding gulls shower kisses on the waves.
We have come home

Where through the lightning flash
And thundering rain
The Pestilence, the drought
The sodden spirit
Lingers on the sandy road
Supporting the tortured remnants
Of the flesh
That spirit which asks no favour
But to have dignity.

One Long Jump

One long jump
From the early days
When the face was like a globe
Round, revolving, limitless
Sharp incisive like a probe
And eyes which could see
With the completeness of a globe – geometrically
A soft film of brown hairs
And a language of birds and flowers.

One long jump
From the early days
When wave upon wave
Of passion merged
Cutting their losses
Preserving their 'gains'
And beauty tingled the flesh
Like a snake
On the surface of the lake
Yielding her store of comfort
Without deceit
Without fictitious powers of support
And no didactic analyses
To know that milk was sweet.

One long jump
And never another
Never quite the same
Because things get mouldy
In the grave
and milk loses its taste
On the coated tongue
Bartered birthrite
Like the chaste membrane
Is lost for good
So we can never arrive
At the beginning
To couch in the blue light
Of the primaeval hive
Except in the dissolution of the flesh
And early strength never returns
To oppose the grinding artificialities
Or to marvel at the rose

One long jump
The first and last
And no progression
So take it well.
Looking back upsets
The balanced wheel
Too tired if we arrive

It is enough
To seek the short cut
To the grave.

Parachute Men

Parachute Men say
The first jump
Takes the breath away
Feet in the air disturbs
Till you get used to it.

Solid ground
Is not where you left it
As you plunge down
Perhaps head first
As you listen to
Your arteries talking
You learn to sustain hope

Suddenly you are only
Holding an open umbrella
In a windy place
As the warm earth
Reaches out to you
Reassures you
The vibrating interim is over

You try to land
Where the green grass yields
And carry your pack
Across the fields.

The violent arrival
Puts out the joint
Earth has nowhere to go
You are at the starting point

Jumping across worlds
In condensed time
After the awkward fall
We are always at the starting point.

Isatou Died

Isatou died
When she was only five
And full of pride
Just before she knew
How small a loss
It brought to such a few.
Her mother wept
Half grateful
To be so early bereft.
And did not see the smile
As tender as the root
Of the emerging plant
Which sealed her eyes.
The neighbours wailed
As they were paid to do
And thought how big a spread
Might be her wedding too.
The father looked at her
Through marble eyes and said;
'Who spilt the perfume
Mixed with morning dew?'

Ghana

Ellis Ayitey Komey

The Change

Your infancy now a wall of memory
In harmattan the locusts filled the sky
Destroying the sweat put into the field
And restless seas shattered canoes
The fisher-folk put to sail by noon.
The impatience in your teens
Yet silent were your dreams
With the fires in your heart
Breaking the mask of innocence.
The evasive solitude in your womb
And the determination of your limbs
With eyes like the soaring eagle
Shattering the glass of ignorance.
Your infancy now a wall of memory
Before this you, like the worms,
Leaning on for vain indecorous dreams
And the cobras with venomous tongues
Licking the tepid blooms of hibiscus

Oblivion

I want to remember the fallen palm
With whitening fluid of wine
Dripping from its hardened belly
In this forest of life.

I want to remember it from the road
With mud on my feet,
And thorn-scraped flesh
From the branches by the water.

I want to remember them well
The sight of the green-eyed forest
The jubilant voices of the frogs
And the pleading cries of the owls.

I want to walk among the palms
With their razor-edged leaves
Shadowing the yam and cassava shrubs
Under which the crab builds its castle
And the cocoa pods drooping like mothers
Breasts feeding a hungry child.

I want to remember them all
Before they die and turn to mud
When I have gone.

Kwesi Brew

A Plea for Mercy

We have come to your shrine to worship –
We the sons of the land.
The naked cowherd has brought
The cows safely home,
And stands silent with his bamboo flute
Wiping the rain from his brow;
As the birds brood in their nests
Awaiting the dawn with unsung melodies;
The shadows crowd on the shores
Pressing their lips against the bosom of the sea;
The peasants home from their labours
Sit by their log fires
Telling tales of long ago.
Why should we the sons of the land
Plead unheeded before your shrine,
When our hearts are full of song
And our lips tremble with sadness?
The little firefly vies with the star,
The log fire with the sun
The water in the calabash
With the mighty Volta.
But we have come in tattered penury
Begging at the door of a Master.

The Search

The past
Is but the cinders
Of the present;
The future
The smoke
That escaped
Into the cloud-bound sky.

Be gentle, be kind my beloved
For words become memories,
And memories tools
In the hands of jesters.
When wise men become silent,
It is because they have read
The palms of Christ
In the face of the Buddha.

So look not for wisdom
And guidance
In their speech, my beloved.
Let the same fire
Which chastened their tongues
Into silence,
Teach us – teach us!

The rain came down,
When you and I slept away
The night's burden of our passions;
Their new-found wisdom
In quick lightning flashes
Revealed the truth
That they had been
The slaves of fools.

Kofi Awoonor

Songs of Sorrow

Dzogbese Lisa has treated me thus
It has led me among the sharps of the forest
Returning is not possible
And going forward is a great difficulty
The affairs of this world are like the chameleon faeces
Into which I have stepped
When I clean it cannot go.*

I am on the world's extreme corner,
I am not sitting in the row with the eminent
But those who are lucky
Sit in the middle and forget
I am on the world's extreme corner
I can only go beyond and forget.

My people, I have been somewhere
If I turn here, the rain beats me
If I turn there the sun burns me
The firewood of this world
Is only for those who can take heart
That is why not all can gather it.
The world is not good for anybody
But you are so happy with your fate;
Alas! the travellers are back
All covered with debt.

Something has happened to me
The things so great that I cannot weep;
I have no sons to fire the gun when I die
And no daughters to wail when I close my mouth
I have wandered on the wilderness

*Colloquial: It [the faeces] will not go [come off].

89

The great wilderness men call life
The rain has beaten me,
And the sharp stumps cut as keen as knives
I shall go beyond and rest.
I have no kin and no brother,
Death has made war upon our house;

And Kpeti's great household is no more,
Only the broken fence stands;
And those who dared not look in his face
Have come out as men.
How well their pride is with them.
Let those gone before take note
They have treated their offspring badly.
What is the wailing for?
Somebody is dead. Agosu himself
Alas! a snake has bitten me
My right arm is broken,
And the tree on which I lean is fallen.

Agosu if you go tell them,
Tell Nyidevu, Kpeti, and Kove
That they have done us evil;
Tell them their house is falling
And the trees in the fence
Have been eaten by termites;
That the martels curse them.
Ask them why they idle there
While we suffer, and eat sand,
And the crow and the vulture
Hover always above our broken fences
And strangers walk over our portion.

Song of War

I shall sleep in white calico;
War has come upon the sons of men
And I shall sleep in calico;
Let the boys go forward,
Kpli and his people should go forward;
Let the white man's guns boom,
We are marching forward;
We all shall sleep in calico.

When we start, the ground shall shake;
The war is within our very huts;
Cowards should fall back
And live at home with the women;
They who go near our wives
While we are away in battle
Shall lose their calabashes when we come.

Where has it been heard before
That a snake has bitten a child
In front of its own mother;
The war is upon us
It is within our very huts
And the sons of men shall fight it
Let the white man's guns boom
And its smoke cover us
We are fighting them to die.

We shall die on the battlefield
We shall like death at no other place,
Our guns shall die with us
And our sharp knives shall perish with us
We shall die on the battlefield.

The Sea Eats the Land at Home

At home the sea is in the town,
Running in and out of the cooking places,
Collecting the firewood from the hearths
And sending it back at night;
The sea eats the land at home.
It came one day at the dead of night,
Destroying the cement walls,
And carried away the fowls,
The cooking-pots and the ladles,
The sea eats the land at home;
It is a sad thing to hear the wails,
And the mourning shouts of the women,
Calling on all the gods they worship,
To protect them from the angry sea.
Aku stood outside where her cooking-pot stood,
With her two children shivering from the cold,
Her hands on her breast,
Weeping mournfully.
Her ancestors have neglected her,
Her gods have deserted her,
It was a cold Sunday morning,
The storm was raging,
Goats and fowls were struggling in the water,
The angry water of the cruel sea;
The lap-lapping of the bark water at the shore,
And above the sobs and the deep and low moans,
Was the eternal hum of the living sea.
It has taken away their belongings
Adena has lost the trinkets which
Were her dowry and her joy,
In the sea that eats the land at home,
Eats the whole land at home.

Three poems from *Rediscovery* (1964)

Lovers' Song

Call her, call her for me, that girl
That girl with the neck like a desert tree
Call her that she and I will lie in one bed.
When you went away
Isn't it seven years?
Shall I fold mine and say I am cheap
Returned unsold from the market
If they marry a woman don't they sleep with her?
Isn't it seven years now since you went away?

The Weaver Bird

The weaver bird built in our house
And laid its eggs on our only tree
We did not want to send it away
We watched the building of the nest
And supervised the egg-laying.
And the weaver returned in the guise of the owner
Preaching salvation to us that owned the house
They say it came from the west
Where the storms at sea had felled the gulls
And the fishers dried their nets by lantern light
Its sermon is the divination of ourselves
And our new horizons limit at its nest
But we cannot join the prayers and answers of the communicants.
We look for new homes every day,
For new altars we strive to rebuild
The old shrines defiled by the weaver's excrement.

Easter Dawn

That man died in Jerusalem
And his death demands dawn marchers
From year to year to the sound of bells.
The hymns flow through the mornings
Heard on Calvary this dawn.

the gods are crying, my father's gods are crying
for a burial – for a final ritual –
but they that should build the fallen shrines
have joined the dawn marchers
singing their way towards Gethsemane
where the tear drops of agony still freshen the cactus.
He has risen! Christ has risen!
the gods cried again from the hut in me
asking why that prostration has gone unheeded.
The marchers sang of the resurrection
That concerned the hillock of Calvary
Where the ground at the foot of the cross is level.
the gods cried, shedding
clayey tears on the calico
the drink offering had dried up in the harmattan
the cola-nut is shrivelled
the yam feast has been eaten by mice
and the fetish priest is dressing for the Easter service.
The resurrection hymns come to me from afar
touching my insides.
Then the gods cried loudest
Challenging the hymners.
They seized their gongs and drums
And marched behind the dawn marchers
Seeking their Calvary
Seeking their tombstones
And those who refused to replace them
In the appropriate season.

From *Night of My Blood* (1971)

At the Gates

I do not know which god sent me,
to fall in the river
and fall in the fire.
These have failed.
I move into the gates
demanding which war it is;
which war it is?
the dwellers in the gates
answer us; we will let that war come

they whom we followed to come
sons of our own mothers and fathers
bearing upon our heads nothing
save the thunder that does roar
who knows when evil matters will come.

Open the gates!
It is Akpabli Horsu who sent me
Open the gates, my mother's children
and let me enter
our thunder initiates have run amok
and we sleep in the desert land
not moving our feet
we will sleep in the desert
guns in our hands we cannot fire
knives in our hands we cannot throw
the death of a man is not far away.

I will drink it; it is my god who gave it to me
I will drink this calabash
for it is god's gift to me
bachelor, never go too far
for the drummer boys will cook and let you eat.

Don't cry for me
my daughter, death called her
it is an offering of my heart
the ram has not come to stay
three days and it has gone
elders and chiefs whom will I trust
a snake has bitten my daughter
whom will I trust?
walk on gently; give me an offering
that I will give it to God
and he will be happy.

Uproot the yams you planted
for everything comes from God
it is an evil god who sent me
that all I have done
I bear the magic of the singer that has come
I have no paddle, my wish,
to push my boat into the river.

GHANA

From *Ride Me, Memory* (1973)

Afro-American Beats III: An American Memory of Africa

Black as my night, anonymous here
my death in Elizabethville was your death.
Blood shed in Sharpeville was shed before in Ulundi
Alabama, Memphis
Fred Hampton on a Chicago bed
blood and gun fire in darkness
was it prophesied that the panther
shall die in his bed without a leap?
I hug my black skin here against my better judgement
hung my shields and sheaves for a season
Leaving Africa that September 1967
in flight from the dreams we build
in the pale talons of eagles yard
donkeys braying on the bloody field across the square
the bulge of my sails unfurl for the
harbour of hate;
The pride of this colour
by which they insist on defining my objection;
that I am a nigger is no matter
but that I died in Memphis and Elizabethville
outrages my self-esteem
I plot my vengeance silently
like Ellison's men in bright dens
of hiding and desperate anonimity
and with the hurricanes and eagles of tomorrow
prepare a firm and final rebuttal to your lies.
To be delivered in the season of infinite madness.

From *The House by the Sea* (1978)

The First Circle

1

the flat end of sorrow here
two crows fighting over New Year's Party
leftovers. From my cell, I see a cold
hard world.

2

So this is the abscess that
hurts the nation –
jails, torture, blood
and hunger.
One day it will burst;
it must burst.

3

When I heard you were taken
we speculated, those of us at large
where you would be
in what nightmare will you star?
That night I heard the moans
wondering whose child could now
be lost in the cellars of oppression.
Then you emerged, tall, and bloody-eyed.

It was the first time
I wept.

4

      The long nights I dread most
       the voices from behind the bars
       the early glow of dawn before
the guard's steps wake me up,
the desire to leap and stretch
and yawn in anticipation
of another dark home-coming day
only to find that
      I cannot.
       riding the car into town
hemmed in between them
      their guns poking me in the ribs,
      I never had known that my people
      wore such sad faces, so sad
      they were on New Year's Eve,
      so very sad.

Atukwei Okai

999 Smiles
(*to Guy Warren*)

nine hundred and ninety-nine smiles
plus
one quarrel ago, our eyes and our
hearts
were in agreement full that still

The sun rises in the East
And sets in the West, that
Still
Rains fall from above
Downward to the earth
That
Still smokes rise from the
Earth, reaching for the sky
That
Still our earth is round and
Not flat like a spread-out
Mat

and yet . . .
            see where
                        today
you have
            gone
                  to sit . . .
throwing . . .
            stones
                  at us . . .
poisonous . . .
            stones
                  at us . . .
satanic . . .
            stones . . .
                  at us . . .

And if I still had my hands
On my shoulders I should raise
One of my hands above my
Head
And gauge and catch your
Stones, one by one, while they
Were still hot in the cool
Air,

and yet . . .
        see where . . .
                today
you have
      gone
           to sit . . .
hurling . . .
        stones . . .
                at us . . .
hurling . . .
        stones . . .
                at us . . .
infernal . . .
        stones . . .
                at us . . .
sinister . . .
        stones . . .
                at us . . .

But all the same, I shall not even
Utter your name, lest the fast and
Faithful
Winds repeat it to the hearing of
Our ancestors who are asleep
With
Their eyes, but not asleep with
Their ears, lest our ancestors
Angrily
Rise out of their nest and
Breathe out the winds that can
Shake
Till it breaks, the decayed drooping

Branch
upon which
            of all
                    people
you today
        have gone
                    to sit . . .
hurling . . .
            stones . . .
                        at us . . .
wrathful . . .
            stones . . .
                        at us . . .
saddening . . .
            stones . . .
                        at us . . .

Charging precisely to our
Head, and if I still had my
Hands about me, I would
Gather
Your stones into a heap, and
Leave them there to lie till
Some morrow when we might
Use

Them to bring down to the warm
Tongues of some fire, fleshy
Birds, that above our heads are
Perched,
Just like you, upon the slippery
Branch of the air; and if still
I had my hands with me, I would
Catch
And keep your stones without thinking
Of throwing them back at you – but
The hands too soon you have stolen away
With
you
    to where
            today

you have
       gone
            to perch
throwing . . .
          stones . . .
                   at us . . .
venomous . . .
          stones . . .
                   at us . . .
spiteful . . .
          stones . . .
                   at us . . .

nine hundred and ninety-nine smiles
plus
one quarrel ago our eyes and our
hearts
were in agreement full that still

When a man lifts his foot, it is
Forward
That he places it, that still, each
Human
Being owns only ten fingers on two
Hands

Kofi Anyidoho

Hero and Thief

I was counting time in the heartbeat of the storm
when Fui and Enyo came riding through whirlwinds
she with the dream beauty of new rainbows
and he in his quiet way spoke of how
a nervous govt sits on a bankrupt stool
wearing a gown of fantasy and hope
telling tales of foreign aid and godmothers at Christmas time

Is it enough we search the private dreams of poets
when our land's nightmares give birth to strange desires
and our children draw their wishes in the quicksands of this earth?
Is it enough is it enough we probe the pampered dreams of poets
while our people scratch the dunghills of this earth
where once the flowers bloomed and poured perfume
upon the pestilence of rotten memories?
Is it enough is it enough we dream in foreign languages
and drink champagne in banquet halls of a proud people
while our people crack palm kernels with their teeth?
It is not enough it isn't enough
to go in search of the lone hero
while the common thief inherits our ancient stools

There have been thieves before on our land

when the harvest left enough surplus for the thieving hand
and we said the thief never reaps much more than farm owner
But the harvest dance is gone
Our harvest gatherers crawl on empty granary floors
keeping tears away with ancient festive hopes:

> my people, how soon again in our hive shall we swarm around our
> honey-comb?

So the thieving hand has reaped much more than farm owner
and the harvest dream transforms into slow funereal hopes
the rice harvest has gone to weaverbird

103

the corn-on-the-cob has gone to grasscutter
the yam-in-the-mound was carried off by rat
and now we sit and watch the flowering bean and
the ripened fruit of palm being plucked at dawn
by slippery hands of night workers

Tomorrow at noon we'll flock the conference hall
of the academy of sciences and hear the learned talk
on post-harvest perspiration of yam tubers
> Is it enough is it enough to dream the moon and stars
> When this earth we own we can't possess?

Soul in Birthwaters

vi. *Ghosts*

a thousand ghosts haunt our soul in birth waters
this life would drown in blood
hammer falls on anvil of
this head, calabash cracks
scattering braindrops on pathways
offering a broken tale to passers-by

watch revolutions of worlds
load guts of goats with power of
bulls, the fools we were
we would seek refuge on wings of their visions
deserting the dream we placed among the thorns

they stole our sleep in a daylight siege
and in our brief madness we
exchanged lullabies for anguished cries

we were all away on the farm
when prowlers of night
sneaked into our pillows
oh they would ambush our sleep
and strangle our dream
the vampires! I saw them
they know I saw them when
father sent me home to fetch a little salt

My voice my voice they seek after my voice!
Do not put me to sleep my people.

Guinea

Ahmed Tidjani-Cissé

Home News

'My dear son I am well thanks be to God
I pray for you day and night.'

'My dear brother it's my sad duty to announce
the death of our beloved mother
Which occurred last Sunday
after a short illness.'

'My cousin I've grown a lot
send me some trousers and new shoes.'

'My love, it's now ten years I've been awaiting you
What's keeping you there in the white man's land
think of the trouble you cause us
by such a long absence.'

'My dear friend our country's changing
into a huge shanty-town.
No-one can eat his fill except . . .
Send me a tape-recorder.'

'My dear son it is I your father
I beg you to return to your land
if not you will not have even
the sorrow of recognizing my tomb.'

'My dear nephew, I must tell you
of your father's death
we all hope you'll be able to attend
the forty-days' wake.'

'My dear . . .'
A tear yesterday when the postman passed
Anxiety today in awaiting his return
The abyss of sadness envelops me
When I have no news from home

My soul shrivels a little
When home news tumbles over me.
The other day I made a fleeting boat
Full of home news.
I set it in the water at the wharf of Exile-Overseas.
I went to attend its arrival
at the landing stage of Loneliness-under-Hope.
My boat landed some secret passengers for me
Next day the postman's prophetic hand was
stretched towards me.

'My dear friend, your brother was arrested
last week in reprisal
for your political work against the government
Your family is left without a head
Send me a shirt and a neck-tie.'

Of Colours and Shadows

Royal blue azure blue
The nobility of a colour
to clothe the uncertainty of conditions.
Green-blue turquoise blue
The adornments of nature
scorn the audacities of imitation
they ornament the fleeting hair of the tornado.
Ash grey, dirty grey, iron grey, pearl grey
The metamorphosing power of a colour
which shatters the yokes of comparison.
Sulphur yellow, saffron yellow, golden yellow
Fever can be yellow
Yellow is a self-respecting colour
The yellow of the egg was the beginning
But the respect for a colour is only apparent
when the yellow peril is in question.
Vermilion red, blood red, poppy red
Cardinals' purple is a red
which sends howling the Gehenna of fear.
The purple of Caesars is all-conquering
Cortez and Pizarro have flaunted the colours of Europe
to the redskins in organizing a hecatomb.

Marxism-Leninism is red
There are colours of poverty
fetichist colours
opulent colours
colours which strike terror or which the whole world unfurls.
Milk white kapok white
The moon is white
Innocence is white
the blindman's stick is white
the Ku-Klux-Klan is robed in white
my village was evangelized by the White Fathers.
Their words were transmitted with the aid of white cold steel.
To fashion the centuries of history
men have invented all the nuances of a colour.
Black bread, black night, black misery
Mourning is black, the devil is black
with black ebony one can construct
a black market to supply the fields
with cotton of the whitest fibre.
The colours which compose my rainbow
Have the density of shadows.
At the borders of my rainbow
history has allowed only a clear obscurity to float.
Like a raging cataract
the dusky shadows of my colour
make a rampart around my house
every time I try to break
the barriers of colour.
Red, blue, yellow, white, black.
The shadows of colours are not truly multicoloured.
Red as palm oil
The snow hides in its own whiteness
behind my door
it will not see me
I have ceased to be the shadow of my colour.

Ivory Coast

Joseph Miezan Bognini

From *Ce Dur Appel de l'Espoir* (1960)

My Days Overgrown

My days overgrown with coffee blossoms,
My childhood has lost its meaning.

The hatred one has eaten
Can never be destroyed.

Misfortune, I am misfortune,
And my shadow has betrayed me;
Suffering, I am suffering,
Inexperienced at the breast of mankind.

I wish you were music
Rocking the thirsty hearts from afar.

You will carry me away one day
Wrapped in white robes
Into another world.

I have become a grain of sand
Drifting along trembling beaches.

You will bring me asylum
That knows the pain of this night.

You changed your face,
I took you by the hand

And we spent happy days.

Earth and Sky

Earth and sky are infinities
Where our cries cannot venture

I have fixed my head between two stones
Seeking the Shelterer in vain.

Only your splendour sets me free

I have run through the void
Crossing a thousand villages

Where could I draw breath
Without damaging your scenery?

The nights have flayed me
Like a careless wanderer.

I am simply an insect
Without wings or paws

Scornful serpents are my only fare

Heat crackles upon my roof
The ripe fruit of my flesh is shrinking

Love lies crumpled at my feet.
I would strip myself of all my cares
And wear the dress of consolation only.

Such joy is new to me.

I will take you for my companion
My body is lost in your arms.

But make me insensate as the wind
Which strikes and ravages nature,
Not to make me hate you
But to love you always.

Two poems from *Herbe Féconde* (1973)

1

We are men of the new world a tree prompts us to harmony
A tree whose fruit is pulpy
It isn't the tree of good or evil but that of concupiscence.
Whose fruit was flung on our shoulders at the dawn of our solicitude
and ranged at evening in the freezing spaces of an infallible cuisine!
The silence plays with us. And our aptitudes in this time seized with
firmness rejoice at an audience stooped before the reason justice
triumphantly brandishes.
We are men of the intensest heat
Matter fashioned from resonance
Multiplied souls
Lanterns of immortal light
Lands of unutterable representation

2

Suddenly an old man on the threshold of the age. A wind comes to
swell the despoiled year.
White sands with brownish stocks, Roots excited by the heat.
Delirious paths where the night's hypnosis flies;
I prop myself for a moment on the slope of his pure face and turn my
body
My lamb's vehemence in the suave musicality of his decayed loins
and it is fidelity which pricks the awakening skin
Abundance of fluid which spurs the nuptial dance:
The peasant dreams of his cabbage feet
The epicurean walker swifter than the wind
The crowd explodes with joy and eulogies
Passage of tender gleams under the storm, the skylight opens upon a
lucrative seeding
The granaries will protect their fortunes
I glimpse a luminous ending
Like an alleged transmission
And the bonds of survival offered forever
Sustenance will attain the summit of intensity
Suddenly the old man on the threshold of the age hoists with his
superb hand the leaf of spontaneity.

115

Charles Nokan

My Head is Immense

My head is immense
I have a toad's eyes
A horn stands on the nape of my neck
But a magical music surges
from me.
What tree exhales such rare
perfume?
Dark beauty, how can you spring
from a toad's wallow? How can you
flow from lonely ugliness?
You who look on, you think
that the voice of my instrument
buys my freedom, that I am fluidity, thought
which flies.
No, there is nothing in me
but a pool of sadness.

Kenya

Khadambi Asalache

Death of a Chief

pavements lined
sorrowful silence
tears
the coffin off to somewhere
in black
behind it the entire district
involved
in songs of grief
that flow and follow
a trailing gesture
thoughts
battered syllables
on lips

as past periods
return
in the farewell
of the blank faces
to float a fable
dreams
years of his reign

the path is silent
to this procession
walking into a myth
as he passes
alone
freed from praises
the worldly notion
the sensate achievement that floats
on tongues like a wind
like changeable news

this slow walk seems
a readjustment
from his life
a transit
a sampling of the fragrance
of death and the surprise of
its calm
an eternal grip
cold

Jonathan Kariara

A Leopard Lives in a Muu Tree

A leopard lives in a Muu tree
Watching my home
My lambs are born speckled
My wives tie their skirts tight
And turn away –
Fearing mottled offspring.
They bathe when the moon is high
Soft and fecund
Splash cold mountain stream water on their nipples
Drop their skin skirts and call obscenities.
I'm besieged
I shall have to cut down the Muu tree
I'm besieged
I walk about stiff
Stroking my loins.
A leopard lives outside my homestead
Watching my women
I have called him elder, the one-from-the-same-womb
He peers at me with slit eyes
His head held high
My sword has rusted in the scabbard.
My wives purse their lips
When owls call for mating
I'm besieged
They fetch cold mountain water
They crush the sugar cane
But refuse to touch my beer horn.
My fences are broken
My medicine bags torn
The hair on my loins is singed
The upright post at the gate has fallen
My women are frisky
The leopard arches over my homestead
Eats my lambs
Resuscitating himself.

Jared Angira

If

a squirrel crosses my way
while on a trip
then luck is mine
but when it's a cheetah
or wild cat that crosses there
I turn and go back.

I knock my right foot on stone
while on a trip
I melt in joy
since I shall be overfed
but when it's the left
I turn and go back.

I slip in my shirt
the inside coming out
I jump in merriment
for I shall be overfed.

the first being
I meet in the feeble dawn
is an old woman
I turn to my blanket
it's all ill luck

I dream my relative dead
in midst of sweet slumbers
I wake in joy
knowing he's overfed
the previous night
and if I dream I am dead
I rejoice
for growing an inch.
and if I dream
of my ideal girl

then I lose hope
the answer is no.

I wake up in the morning
and find my teeth shaking
and loose
surely I know
they went eating excreta
while soul courted in fairyland.

A hen crows
it must be killed
bad omen
a dog howls
instead of barking
the village owner
is at death's door
and if I walk on my head
then I am dead.

The Country of the Dead

The country of the dead
I speak
no answer
I weep
no pity
I watch
no colour
I listen
no sound
the country of the dead

I shout, the echo strikes
the dead rock
I kick, my toe mutilates
on dry stump
I weep, no pity
the country of the dead

I've searched the exit
but heard no owls

no parrots, the waves beat afar
on wrecks of ships
the sand stares with me
the country of the dead.

Manna

So all waited for manna
In the orange dawn
And let their feet
Crack in the dew

No one bothered to ask
The labourers
To bring forth this manna

Many said
A miracle recorded
For God never laboured

The first shipment
Of this manna
Landed to a clean swept spot
And many wide throated waiters
Never chanced to see it.

Children wailed in hunger
Idle mothers rushed
To the screening chamber
Even mothers
Who had worked
Mighty hard
Sank in the scrum

Soon the manna craft
Took off from ground
And hungry natives
Soared the sky
But they only saw
The rainbow
Which promised them
Hunger in seven days
Death in seven ways.

A Look in the Past

Once I was a lizard
cheeky and harmless
and built clouds
that the heat
never could melt

I learnt
of the transanimation
into a monitor
deaf to all spikes
a dweller of two worlds . . .

ere my breath had settled
my back grew rough –
my teeth went chisel-like
. . . a crocodile
lurking in sandy seafloor

then one day I died
but knocked my head
on the sharp gravestone
that woke me up
to find me winged
tough-clawed and a scavenger . . .
I was an eagle.

I went on sojourn
and my red eyes blue'ed
till I turned priestly –
pigeoned
till we came to Guernica
where they pinched my olive branch
and gave me a bone

when next I stopped
I was gliding
mutilated . . .
the mongoose pursued me in hideways

I shall go back
to the formless clouds
and melt myself into rain

then shall I land in the plantation
and mate with the secondary roots
of the old fig tree.

Request

Open your palms
to form a jar
and pour there water
to quench the thirst

Open your throat
and form a fan
to blow it over
and cool the panting soul

Burst open the gates
of that home
where Jove
lies in majesty
of loneliness

Tear off the curtain
of the window
on the facade
of satisfaction
and pass me through
to the honeyed comb

Open your bosom
and release
the juice
denied a seedling
below the brassieres

Coil your tongue
Aloo
Aloo
ignite your yellow breath
and let me pass
to the honeyed comb.

Madagascar

Jean-Joseph Rabéarivelo

Four poems from *Traduits de la Nuit*

2

What invisible rat
come from the walls of night
gnaws at the milky cake of the moon?
Tomorrow morning,
when it has gone,
there will be bleeding marks of teeth.

Tomorrow morning
those who have drunk all night
and those who have abandoned their cards,
blinking at the moon
will stammer out:
'Whose is that sixpence
that rolls over the green table?'
'Ah!' one of them will add,
'our friend has lost everything
and killed himself!'

And all will snigger
and, staggering, will fall.
The moon will no longer be there:
the rat will have carried her into his hole.

3

The hide of the black cow is stretched,
stretched but not set to dry,
stretched in the sevenfold shadow.
But who has killed the black cow,
dead without having lowed, dead without having roared,
dead without having once been chased
over that prairie flowered with stars?

She who calves in the far half of the sky.

Stretched is the hide
on the sounding-box of the wind
that is sculptured by the spirits of sleep.

And the drum is ready
when the new-born calf,
her horns crowned with spear grass
leaps
and grazes the grass of the hills.

It reverberates there
and its incantations will become dreams
until the moment when the black cow lives again,
white and pink
before a river of light.

14

She
whose eyes are prisms of sleep
and whose lids are heavy with dreams,
she whose feet are planted in the sea
and whose shiny hands appear
full of corals and blocks of shining salt.

She will put them in little heaps beside a misty gulf
and sell them to naked sailors
whose tongues have been cut out,
until the rain begins to fall.

Then she will disappear
and we shall only see
her hair spread by the wind
like a bunch of seaweed unravelling,
and perhaps some tasteless grains of salt.

18

The black glassmaker
whose countless eyeballs none has ever seen,
whose shoulders none has overlooked,
that slave all clothed in pearls of glass,
who is strong as Atlas
and who carries the seven skies on his head,
one would think that the vast river of clouds might carry him away,
the river in which his loincloth is already wet.

A thousand particles of glass
fall from his hands
but rebound towards his brow
shattered by the mountains
where the winds are born.

And you are witness of his daily suffering
and of his endless task;
you watch his thunder-riddled agony
until the battlements of the East re-echo
the conches of the sea –
but you pity him no more
and do not even remember that his sufferings begin again
each time the sun capsizes.

Cactus

(from *Presque-songes*)

That multitude of moulded hands
holding out flowers to the azure sky
that multitude of fingerless hands
unshaken by the wind
they say that a hidden source
wells from their untainted palms
they say that this inner source
refreshes thousands of cattle
and numberless tribes, wandering tribes
in the frontiers of the South.

Fingerless hands, springing from a source,
Moulded hands, crowning the sky.

Here, when the flanks of the City were still as green
as moonbeams glancing from the forests,
when they still left bare the hills of Iarive
crouching like bulls upthrust,
it was upon rocks too steep even for goats
that they hid, to protect their sources,
these lepers sprouting flowers.

Enter the cave from which they came
if you seek the origin of the sickness which ravages them –
origin more shrouded than the evening
and further than the dawn –
but you will know no more than I.
The blood of the earth, the sweat of the stone,
and the sperm of the wind,
which flow together in these palms
have melted their fingers
and replaced them with golden flowers.

Flavien Ranaivo

Song of a Young Girl

Oaf
the young man who lives down there
beside the threshing floor for rice;
like two banana-roots
on either side the village ditch,
we gaze on each other,
we are lovers,
but he won't marry me.
Jealous
his mistress I saw two days since at the wash house
coming down the path against the wind.
She was proud;
was it because she wore a lamba thick
and studded with coral
or because they are newly bedded?
However it isn't the storm
that will flatten the delicate reed,
nor the great sudden shower
at the passage of a cloud
that will startle out of his wits
the blue bull.
I am amazed;
the big sterile rock
survived the rain of the flood
and it's the fire that crackles
the bad grains of maize.
Such this famous smoker
who took tobacco
when there was no more hemp to burn.
A foot of hemp?
– Sprung in Andringitra,
spent in Ankaratra,
no more than cinders to us.

False flattery
stimulates love a little
but the blade has two edges;
why change what is natural?
– If I have made you sad
look at yourself in the water of repentance,
you will decipher there a word I have left.
Good-bye, whirling puzzle,
I give you my blessing:
wrestle with the crocodile,
here are your victuals and three water-lily flowers
for the way is long.

Song of a Common Lover

Don't love me, my dear,
like your shadow
for shadows fade at evening
and I want to keep you
right up to cockcrow;
nor like pepper
which makes the belly hot
for then I couldn't take you
when I'm hungry;
nor like a pillow
for we'd be together in the hours of sleep
but scarcely meet by day;
nor like rice
for once swallowed you think no more of it;
nor like soft speeches
for they quickly vanish;
nor like honey,
sweet indeed but too common.
Love me like a beautiful dream,
your life in the night,
my hope in the day;
like a piece of money,
ever with me on earth,
and for the great journey
a faithful comrade;
like a calabash:
intact, for drawing water;
in pieces, bridges for my guitar.

Malawi

David Rubadiri

An African Thunderstorm

From the west
Clouds come hurrying with the wind
Turning
Sharply
Here and there
Like a plague of locusts
Whirling
Tossing up things on its tail
Like a madman chasing nothing.

Pregnant clouds
Ride stately on its back
Gathering to perch on hills
Like dark sinister wings;
The Wind whistles by
And trees bend to let it pass.

In the village
Screams of delighted children
Toss and turn
In the din of whirling wind,
Women –
Babies clinging on their backs –
Dart about
In and out
Madly
The Wind whistles by
Whilst trees bend to let it pass.
Clothes wave like tattered flags
Flying off
To expose dangling breasts
As jaggered blinding flashes
Rumble, tremble, and crack
Amidst the smell of fired smoke
And the pelting march of the storm.

Felix Mnthali

My Father

That we may have life
and have it abundantly
he endured
the chrome-dust
the damp hell
of Selukwe Peak Mines
the pittance
of American multi-nationals –

They thought it was the watch
on which they had inscribed his name
'for a long and meritorious service'
that made him beam . . .
they never saw blacks
as men with ambition
but only as a 'labour force'
the long arm of their
'manifest destiny',
the vital source
of their strategic metals.

He smiled
    smiled because one day
    one day . . .
    his sons would return!

The Stranglehold of English Lit.
(*for Molara Ogundipe-Leslie*)

Those questions, sister,
those questions
         stand
         stab
         jab
      and gore
too close to the centre!

For if we had asked
why Jane Austen's people
carouse all day
and do no work

would Europe in Africa
have stood
the test of time?
and would she still maul
the flower of our youth
in the south?
Would she?

Your elegance of deceit,
Jane Austen,
lulled the sons and daughters
of the dispossessed
into a calf-love
with irony and satire
around imaginary people.

While history went on mocking
the victims of branding irons
and sugar-plantations
that made Jane Austen's people
wealthy beyond compare!

Eng. Lit., my sister,
was more than a cruel joke –
it was the heart
of alien conquest.

How could questions be asked
at Makerere and Ibadan,
Dakar and Ford Hare –
with Jane Austen
at the centre?
How could they be answered?

The Celebration

Before bulging eyes
a cacoon breaks
and its worm spits
the venom of vipers!

Gliding kingfishers
muster
the fury of a hawk;
saplings and ferns brood
like baobabs in the Rift Valley;
from the back of nowhere
waifs prophesy
the day of judgement.

We have bedecked with flowers
gun-carriers, guns and bayonets;
filled gourds with honey
from mountains belching fire –

It is while it lasts,
the hour of revelation,
the well-spring of love and hate,
a celebration!

Jack Mapanje

Before Chilembwe Tree

1

Didn't you say we should trace
your footprints unmindful of
quagmires, thickets and rivers
until we reached your *nsolo* tree?

Now, here I seat my gourd of beer
on my little fire throw my millet
flour and my smoked meat while
I await the second coming.

2

Why does your mind boggle:
Who will offer another gourd
Who will force another step
To hide our shame?

The goat blood on the rocks
The smoke that issued
The drums you danced to
And the rains hoped for –

You've chanted yourselves hoarse
Chilembwe is gone in your dust
Stop lingering then:
Who will start another fire?

On Being Asked to Write a Poem for 1979

Without kings and warriors occasional verse fails

Skeletal Kampuchea children staring, cold
Stubborn Irish children throwing grenades
These are objects too serious for verse,
Crushed Soweto children clutching their entrails
Then in verse bruised, mocks

Today no poet sufficiently asks why dying children
Stare or throw bombs. And why should we
Compute painful doubts that will forever occupy us?
Talking oil-crises in our eight-cylinder cars
Is enough travesty . . .

The year of the child must make no difference then
Where tadpoles are never allowed to grow into frogs!

An Elegy for Mangochi Fishermen

Today even those fireflies have become
The banners for our night fishermen
The crabs and *dondolos* dare not
Peep out of their crevices.

The virgin canoe we once boasted about
Holding the head or pushing the rear
Pulling the lips or rolling on poles,
The canoe has capsized, the carvers drowned.

Those loin-cloths dripping, the muscles
Twitching with power, the husky voices chanting
About the delicious chambo dishes expected
Even the toes we once crushed dragging
Our canoe from the arid Namizimu mountains
To the soft beaches of this golden lake –

We will not cast in tender herbs to cure.
Today, you gone, the vigil wax has melted away
The light is out in our cryptic recesses
We must all lie in pitch dark stakes.

Should we then wipe our sticky brows
In the heat of another October? Should we fell
More poles to roll another canoe to the beach?
Is it worth it assembling another voice?

At the Metro: Old Irrelevant Images
(for Blaise)

They are still so anthropologically tall here
Still treating you in irrelevant tribal metaphors:
Somalis have softer skins, they drink milk; they say
(And yours is cracking, you drink *kachasu*!)

Even the most knowledgeable still slip back
Apologizing to you in banal Tarzan images:
The children still know mostly Tarzans at school; they say
(Tarzans choked me too in the fifties, damn it!)

But the College girls' sit-in about rapists was
A bit of a change, and Mrs Thatcher's et cetera
Against overseas students; and, the publisher's dinner!
(How are the jacarandas I left blooming, otherwise?)

The Cheerful Girls at Smiller's Bar, 1971

The prostitutes at Smiller's Bar beside the dusty road
Were only girls once in tremulous mini-skirts and oriental
Beads, cheerfully swigging Carlsbergs and bouncing to
Rusty simanje-manje and rumba booming in the juke-box.
They were striking virgins bored by our Presbyterian
Prudes until a true Presbyterian came one night. And like
To us all the girls offered him a seat on cheap planks
In the dark backyard room choked with diesel-oil clouds
From a tin-can lamp. Touched the official rolled his eyes
To one in style. She said no. Most girls only wanted
A husband to hook or the fruits of Independence to taste
But since then mini-skirts were banned and the girls
Of Smiller's Bar became 'ugly prostitutes to boot!'

Today the girls still giggle about what came through
The megaphones: the preservation of our traditional
et cetera . . .

Mali

Ouologuem Yambo

When Negro Teeth Speak

Everyone thinks me a cannibal
But you know how people talk

Everyone sees my red gums but who
Has white ones
Up with tomatoes

Everyone says fewer tourists will come
Now
But you know
We aren't in America and anyway everyone
Is broke

Everyone says it's my fault and is afraid
But look
My teeth are white not red
I haven't eaten anyone

People are wicked and say I gobble
the tourists roasted
Or perhaps grilled
Roasted or grilled I asked them
They fell silent and looked fearfully at my gums
Up with tomatoes

Everyone knows an arable country has agriculture
Up with vegetables

Everyone maintains that vegetables
Don't nourish the grower well
And that I am well-grown for an undeveloped man
Miserable vermin living on tourists
Down with my teeth

Everyone suddenly surrounded me
Fettered
Thrown down prostrated
At the feet of justice

Cannibal or not cannibal
Speak up
Ah you think yourself clever
And try to look proud

Now we'll see you get what's coming to you
What is your last word
Poor condemned man

I shouted up with tomatoes

The men were cruel and the women curious you see
There was one in the peering circle
Who with her voice rattling like the lid of a casserole
Screamed
Yelped
Open him up
I'm sure papa is still inside

The knives being blunt
Which is understandable among vegetarians
Like the Westerners
They grabbed a Gillette blade
And patiently
Crisss
Crasss
Floccc
They opened my belly

A plantation of tomatoes was growing there
Irrigated by streams of palm wine
Up with tomatoes

Mauretania

Oumar Ba

Justice is Done

Beaten up,
Robbed,
Hospitalized?
And the witnesses?
Many as grains of the sand:
Kadiel is one;
Ndoulla
Ndyam Bele is one
Even the birds can testify . . .
But you forget that the chief
Has his son as the judge
And his son-in-law as interpreter.

Familiar Oxen

You tell me you have right on your side?
And those oxen that I see
In the chief's herd?
If I call them
They will respond to their baptismal names.

The Ox-Soldier

Don't you know
That an ox of seven seasons
Can become a soldier
And take your place for military service?

Nobility

One musn't confuse the day and the night;
Nor even the fingers
Which are distinguished by their breadth and height.
Neither use of your language
Nor uniform
Bestows power, or birth, or character
On the son of a slave.
You have abolished slavery
Just to subjugate us
To the offspring of our captives.
Commander,
I am the son of my father
Who died in that prison.
France, they say, is justice.
But they see us without eyes,
Through the eyes of others
Billahi! seven times Billahi!
Drive from your service
Those tailless dogs!
Listen to those who do not love you
But whose word is invulnerable
As the centenarian caïlcedrat
Of Salde.
You will have the truth.

Mauritius

Edouard Maunick

Two poems from *Les Manèges de la Mer* (1964)

6

Further off is the measured force the word of the sea
Further without leeway for the blueing shoulders of the horizon

harm is born of the light
when it capsizes under the voyages' assault
when it watches oblivion like a beast
and seeks the shipwreck of ten-year old villages
conclusive shifts of time in exile

further off is risk without defeat
the ever renewed patience of the shadow
to find words beyond language
further the serpent in the blood
broken by all the betrayals
victories of voluntary resignation

I did not leave in order to forget
I am mulatto
the Indian ocean will never give way to the city of today
but harm compromises in me harm however come by

I repeat further off to stain the liquid mirrors
to cross a threshold where you await me since the poem

20

I love to encounter you in strange cities
where every broil every noise every clock
betrays your body beating in my pulses

MAURITIUS

I love to release you in foreign beds
when night becomes a tree by the force of its nudity

I love what separates us in our resemblance
frontiers of dawn resembling our faces
the proofs of life are only found elsewhere
never say no when I speak to you from afar . . .

Mozambique

José Craveiriñha

The Seed is in Me

Dead or living
the seed is in me
in the universal whiteness of my bones

All feel
uneasiness
at the undoubted whiteness of my bones
white as the breasts of Ingrids or Marias
in Scandinavian lands
or in Polana the smart quarter
of my old native town.

All feel
uneasiness
that the mingling in my veins should be
blood from the blood of every blood
and instead of the peace ineffable of pure and simple birth
and a pure and simple death
breed a rash of complexes
from the seed of my bones.

But a night with the massaleiras heavy with green fruit
batuques swirl above the sweating stones
and the tears of rivers

All feel
uneasiness
at the white seed in me
breeding a rash inflamed with malediction.

And one day
will come all the Marias of the distant nations
penitent or no
weeping
laughing
or loving to the rhythm of a song

To say to my bones
forgive us, brother.

Three Dimensions

In the cabin . . .
the god of the machine
in cap and overalls
holds in his hand the secret of the pistons.

In the carriage . . .
the first-class god
elaborates his schemes in regulated air.

And on the branch-line . . .
– feet flat against the steel of the coaches –
bursting his lungs
the god of the trolley.

Noémia de Sousa

Appeal

Who has strangled the tired voice
of my forest sister?
On a sudden, her call to action
was lost in the endless flow of night and day.
No more it reaches me every morning,
wearied with long journeying,
mile after mile drowned
in the everlasting cry: Macala!

No, it comes no more, still damp with dew,
leashed with children and submission....
One child on her back, another in her womb
– always, always, always!
And a face all compassed in a gentle look,
whenever I recall that look I feel
my flesh and blood swell tremulous,
throbbing to revelations and affinities....
– But who has stopped her immeasurable look
from feeding my deep hunger after comradeship
that my poor table never will serve to satisfy?

Io mamane, who can have shot the noble voice
of my forest sister?
What mean and brutal rhino-whip
has lashed until it killed her?

– In my garden the seringa blooms.
But with an evil omen in its purple flower,
in its intense inhuman scent;
and the wrap of tenderness spread by the sun
over the light mat of petals
has waited since summer for my sister's child
to rest himself upon it....

In vain, in vain,
a chirico sings and sings perched among the garden reeds,
for the little boy of my missing sister,
the victim of the forest's vaporous dawns.
Ah, I know, I know: at the last there was a glitter
of farewell in those gentle eyes,
and her voice came like a murmur hoarse.
tragic and despairing....

O Africa, my motherland, answer me:
What was done to my forest sister,
that she comes no more to the city with her eternal little ones
(one on her back, one in her womb),
with her eternal charcoal-vendor's cry?
O Africa, my motherland,
you at least will not forsake my heroic sister,
she shall live in the proud memorial of your arms!

If You Want to Know Me

If you want to know who I am,
examine with careful eyes
that piece of black wood
which an unknown Maconde brother
with inspired hands
carved and worked
in distant lands to the North.

Ah, she is who I am:
empty eye sockets despairing of possessing life
a mouth slashed with wounds of anguish,
enormous, flattened hands,
raised as though to implore and threaten,
body tattooed with visible and invisible scars
by the hard whips of slavery ...
tortured and magnificent,
proud and mystical,
Africa from head to toe,
– ah, she is who I am!

If you want to understand me
come and bend over my African soul,
in the groans of the Negroes on the docks
in the frenzied dances of the Chopes
in the rebelliousness of the Shanganas
in the strange melancholy evaporating
from a native song, into the night . . .

And ask me nothing more
if you really wish to know me . . .
for I am no more than a shell of flesh
in which the revolt of Africa congealed
its cry swollen with hope

Valente Malangatana

To the Anxious Mother

Into your arms I came
when you bore me, very anxious
you, who were so alarmed
at that monstrous moment
fearing that God might take me.
Everyone watched in silence
to see if the birth was going well
everyone washed their hands
to be able to receive the one who came from Heaven
and all the women were still and afraid.
But when I emerged
from the place where you sheltered me so long
at once I drew my first breath
at once you cried out with joy
the first kiss was my grandmother's.
And she took me at once to the place
where they kept me, hidden away
everyone was forbidden to enter my room
because everyone smelt bad
and I all fresh, fresh
breathed gently, wrapped in my napkins.
But grandmother, who seemed like a madwoman,
always looking and looking again
because the flies came at me
and the mosquitoes harried me
God who also watched over me
was my old granny's friend.

Woman

In the cool waters of the river
we shall have fish that are huge
which shall give the sign of
the end of the world perhaps
because they will make an end of woman
woman who adorns the fields
woman who is the fruit of man.

The flying fish makes an end of searching
because woman is the gold of man
when she sings she ever seems
like the fado-singer's well-tuned guitar
when she dies, I shall cut off
her hair to deliver me from sin.

Woman's hair shall be the blanket
over my coffin when another Artist
calls me to Heaven to paint me
woman's breasts shall be my pillow
woman's eye shall open up for me the way to heaven
woman's belly shall give birth to me up there
and woman's glance shall watch me
as I go up to Heaven.

Jorge Rebelo

Poem

Come, brother, and tell me your life
come, show me the marks of revolt
   which the enemy left on your body

Come, say to me 'Here
my hands have been crushed
because they defended
the land which they own'

'Here my body was tortured
because it refused to bend
to invaders'

'Here my mouth was wounded
because it dared to sing
my people's freedom'

Come brother and tell me your life,
come relate me the dreams of revolt
which you and your fathers and forefathers
dreamed
in silence
through shadowless nights made for love

Come tell me these dreams become
war,
the birth of heroes,
land reconquered,
mothers who, fearless,
send their sons to fight.

Come, tell me all this, my brother.

And later I will forge simple words
which even the children can understand
words which will enter every house
like the wind
and fall like red hot embers
on our people's souls.

In our land
Bullets are beginning to flower.

Poem for a Militant

Mother.
I have an iron rifle
your son,
the one you saw chained
one day
(When you cried as if
the chains bound and battered
your hands and feet)
Your boy is free now
Mother.
Your boy has an iron rifle,
My rifle
will break the chains
will open the prisons
will kill the tyrants
will win back our land
Mother,
Beauty is to fight for freedom,
Justice rings in my every shot
and ancient dreams awaken like birds.
Fighting, on the front,
Your image descends.
I fight for you,
Mother
to dry the tears
of your eyes.

Nigeria

Gabriel Okara

The Snowflakes Sail Gently Down

The snowflakes sail gently
down from the misty eye of the sky
and fall lightly lightly on the
winter-weary elms. And the branches
winter-stripped and nude, slowly
with the weight of the weightless snow
bow like grief-stricken mourners
as white funeral cloth is slowly
unrolled over deathless earth.
And dead sleep stealthily from the
heater rose and closed my eyes with
the touch of silk cotton on water falling.

Then I dreamed a dream
in my dead sleep. But I dreamed
not of earth dying and elms a vigil
keeping. I dreamed of birds, black
birds flying in my inside, nesting
and hatching on oil palms bearing suns
for fruits and with roots denting the
uprooters' spades. And I dreamed the
uprooters tired and limp, leaning on my roots –
their abandoned roots
and the oil palms gave them each a sun.

But on their palms
they balanced the blinding orbs
and frowned with schisms on their
brows – for the suns reached not
the brightness of gold!

Then I awoke. I awoke
to the silently falling snow
and bent-backed elms bowing and
swaying to the winter wind like
white-robed Moslems salaaming at evening
prayer, and the earth lying inscrutable
like the face of a god in a shrine.

The Mystic Drum

The mystic drum beat in my inside
and fishes danced in the rivers
and men and women danced on land
to the rhythm of my drum

But standing behind a tree
with leaves around her waist
she only smiled with a shake of her head.

Still my drum continued to beat,
rippling the air with quickened
tempo compelling the quick
and the dead to dance and sing
with their shadows –

But standing behind a tree
with leaves around her waist
she only smiled with a shake of her head.

Then the drum beat with the rhythm
of the things of the ground
and invoked the eye of the sky
the sun and the moon and the river gods –
and the trees began to dance,
the fishes turned men
and men turned fishes
and things stopped to grow –

But standing behind a tree
with leaves around her waist
she only smiled with a shake of her head.

And then the mystic drum
in my inside stopped to beat –
and men became men,
fishes became fishes
and trees, the sun and the moon
found their places, and the dead
went to the ground and things began to grow.

And behind the tree she stood
with roots sprouting from her
feet and leaves growing on her head
and smoke issuing from her nose
and her lips parted in her smile
turned cavity belching darkness.

Then, then I packed my mystic drum
and turned away; never to beat so loud any more.

Adhiambo

I hear many voices
like it's said a madman hears;
I hear trees talking
like it's said a medicine man hears.

Maybe I'm a madman,
I'm a medicine man.

Maybe I'm mad,
for the voices are luring me,
urging me from the midnight
moon and the silence of my desk
to walk on wave crests across a sea.

Maybe I'm a medicine man
hearing talking saps,
seeing behind trees;
but who's lost his powers
of invocation.

But the voices and the trees
are now name-spelling and one figure
silence-etched across

the moonface is walking, stepping
over continents and seas.

And I raised my hand –
my trembling hand, gripping
my heart as handkerchief
and waved and waved – and waved –
but she turned her eyes away.

Spirit of the Wind

The storks are coming now –
white specks in the silent sky.
They had gone north seeking
fairer climes to build their homes
when here was raining.

They are back with me now –
Spirits of the wind,
beyond the gods' confining
hands they go north and west and east,
instinct guiding.

But willed by the gods
I'm sitting on this rock
watching them come and go
from sunrise to sundown, with the spirit
urging within.

And urging a red pool stirs,
and each ripple is
the instinct's vital call,
a desire in a million cells
confined.

O God of the gods and me,
shall I not heed
this prayer-bell call, the noon
angelus, because my stork is caged
in Singed Hair and Dark Skin?

One Night at Victoria Beach

The wind comes rushing from the sea,
the waves curling like mambas strike
the sands and recoiling hiss in rage
washing the Aladuras'* feet pressing hard
on the sand and with eyes fixed hard
on what only hearts can see, they shouting
pray, the Aladuras pray; and coming
from booths behind, compelling highlife
forces ears; and car lights startle pairs
arm in arm passing washer-words back
and forth like haggling sellers and buyers –

Still they pray, the Aladuras pray
with hands pressed against their hearts
and their white robes pressed against
their bodies by the wind; and drinking
palm-wine and beer, the people boast
at bars at the beach. Still they pray.
They pray, the Aladuras pray
to what only hearts can see while dead
fishermen long dead with bones rolling
nibbled clean by nibbling fishes, follow
four dead cowries shining like stars
into deep sea where fishes sit in judgement;
and living fishermen in dark huts
sit round dim lights with Babalawo
throwing their souls in four cowries
on sand, trying to see tomorrow.

Still, they pray, the Aladuras pray
to what only hearts can see behind
the curling waves and the sea, the stars
and the subduing unanimity of the sky
and their white bones beneath the sand.

And standing dead on dead sands,
I felt my knees touch living sands –
but the rushing wind killed the budding words.

* Aladuras: a Christian sect addicted to ritual bathing.

Christopher Okigbo

Seven poems from *Heavensgate* (1961)

Overture

Before you, mother Idoto,
naked I stand,
before your watery presence,
a prodigal,

leaning on an oilbean,
lost in your legend. . . .

Under your power wait I
     on barefoot,
watchman for the watchword
     at heavensgate;

out of the depths my cry
give ear and hearken.

Eyes Watch the Stars

Eyes open on the beach,
eyes open, of the prodigal;
upward to heaven shoot
where stars will fall from.

Which secret I have told into no ear;
     into a dughole to hold,
     not to drown with –
Which secret I have planted into beachsand;

now breaks
salt-white surf on the stones and me,
and lobsters and shells in
iodine smell –
maid of the salt-emptiness,
sophisticreamy, native,

whose secret I have covered up with beachsand.

Shadow of rain
over sunbeaten beach,
shadow of rain
over man with woman.

Water Maid

Bright
with the armpit dazzle of a lioness,
she answers,
wearing white light about her;
and the waves escort her,
my lioness,
crowned with moonlight.

So brief her presence –
match-flare in wind's breath –
so brief with mirrors around me.

Downward . . .
the waves distil her:
gold crop
sinking ungathered.

Watermaid of the salt emptiness,
grown are the ears of the secret.

Sacrifice

Thundering drums and cannons
in palm grove:
the spirit is in ascent.

I have visited,
on palm beam imprinted
my pentagon –

I have visited, the prodigal. . . .

In palm grove
long drums and cannons:
the spirit in the ascent.

Passion Flower

And the flower weeps
        unbruised,
Lacrimae Christi,

For him who was silenced;

        whose advent
dumb bells in the dim light celebrate
        with wine song:

Messiah will come again,
After the argument in heaven;
Messiah will come again,
Lumen mundi. . . .

Fingers of penitence
bring
to a palm grove
vegetable offering
with five
fingers of chalk.

Lustra

So would I to the hills again
so would I
to where springs the fountain
there to draw from
and to hilltop clamber
body and soul
whitewashed in the moondew
there to see from

So would I from my eye the mist
so would I
through moonmist to hilltop
there for the cleansing

Here is a new-laid egg
here a white hen at midterm.

Bridge

I am standing above you and tide
      above the noontide,
Listening to the laughter of waters
      that do not know why:

Listening to incense. . . .

I am standing above the noontide
      with my head above it,
Under my feet float the waters:
      tide blows them under.

Four poems from *Limits* (1962)

Siren Limits

1

Suddenly becoming talkative
      like weaverbird
Summoned at offside of
        dream remembered

Between sleep and waking,
I hang up my egg-shells
To you of palm grove,

Upon whose bamboo towers
Hang, dripping with yesterupwine

A tiger mask and nude spear . . . .

Queen of the damp half-light,
  I have had my cleansing,
Emigrant with airborne nose,
    The he-goat-on-heat.

2

For he was a shrub among the poplars,
Needing more roots
More sap to grow to sunlight,
Thirsting for sunlight

A low growth among the forest.

Into the soul
The selves extended their branches
Into the moments of each living hour
Feeling for audience

Straining thin among the echoes;

And out of the solitude
Voice and soul with selves unite,
Riding the echoes,

Horsemen of the apocalypse,

And crowned with one self
The name displays its foliage,
Hanging low

A green cloud above the forest.

3

Banks of reed.
Mountains of broken bottles.

    & the mortar is not yet dry....

Silent the footfall
soft as cat's paw,
Sandalled in velvet,
     in fur

       So we must go,
Wearing evemist against the shoulders,
Trailing sun's dust sawdust of combat,
With brand burning out at hand-end.

    & the mortar is not yet dry....

       Then we must sing
Tongue-tied without name or audience,
Making harmony among the branches.

And this is the crisis-point,
The twilight moment between
       sleep and waking;
And voice that is reborn transpires
Not thro' pores in the flesh
       but the soul's backbone

Hurry on down
       through the high-arched gate –
Hurry on down
       little stream to the lake;
Hurry on down –
       through the cinder market

Hurry on down
   in the wake of the dream;
Hurry on down –
   To rockpoint of CABLE
   To pull by the rope
   The big white elephant....

  & the mortar is not yet dry
  & the mortar is not yet dry ....

& the dream wakes
  & the voice fades
In the damp half-light,
  Like a shadow,

Not leaving a mark.

4

An image insists
  from the flag-pole of the heart,
The image distracts
  with the cruelty of the rose ....

  My lioness,
(No shield is lead-plate against you)
Wound me with your seaweed face
  Blinded like a strongroom.

Distances of your
  arm-pit fragrance
Turn chloroform,
  enough for my patience –

When you have finished,
& done up my stitches
Wake me near the altar
  & this poem will be finished.

One poem from *Lament of the Drums* (1964)

1

Lion-hearted cedar forest, gonads for our thunder,
Even if you are very far away, we invoke you:

Give us our hollow heads of long-drums ...

Antelopes for the cedar forest, swifter messengers
Than flash-of-beacon-flame, we invoke you:

Hide us; deliver us from our nakedness ...

Many-fingered canebrake, exile for our laughter,
Even if you are very far away, we invoke you:

Come; limber our raw hides of antelopes ...

Thunder of tanks of giant iron steps of detonators,
Fail safe from the clearing, we implore you:

We are tuned for a feast-of-seven-souls ...

Two poems from *Distances* (1964)

1

From flesh into phantom,
on the horizontal stone:

I was the sole witness to my homecoming ...

Serene lights on the other balcony –
redolent fountains, bristling with signs.
But what does my divine rejoicing hold?
A bowl of incense? A nest of fireflies?

I was the sole witness to my homecoming ...

And in the inflorescence of the white chamber,
a voice, from very far away, chanted, and the chamber descanted
the birthday of earth, paddling me home through
some dark labyrinth, from laughter to the dream.

Miner into my solitude, incarnate
voice of the dream, you will go,
with me as your chief acolyte,
again into the ant-hole . . .

I was the sole witness to my homecoming . . .

2

Death lay in ambush,
that evening in that island;
and the voice sought its echo,
that evening in that island,
and the eye lost its light,
and the light lost its shadow.

And the wind, eternal suitor of dead leaves,
unrolled his bandages to the finest swimmer . . .

And it was an evening without flesh or skeleton;
an evening with no silver bells to its tale;
without lanterns; without buntings;
and it was an evening without age or memory –

for we are talking of such commonplace things,
and on the brink of such great events –
and in the freezing tuberoses of the white
chamber, eyes that had lost their animal
colour – havoc of incandescent rays –
pinned me, cold to the marble stretcher,
        until my eyes lost their blood,
            and the blood lost its odour;
and the everlasting fire from the oblong window
forgot the taste of ash in the air's marrow . . .

Anguish and solitude ...
Smothered, my scattered
cry, the dancers,
lost among their own
snares; the faces,
the hands, held captive;
the interspaces
reddening with blood ...

And behind them all,
in smock of white cotton,
Death herself,
the chief celebrant,
in a cloud of incense,
paring her fingernails ...

At her feet roll their heads like cut fruits;
about her fall
their severed members, numerous as locusts.

Like split wood left to dry,
the dismembered joints
of the ministrants pile high.

She bathes her knees in the blood of attendants,
her smock in the entrails of the ministrants ...

From *Come Thunder* (1967)

Come Thunder

Now that the triumphant march has entered the last street corners,
Remember, O dancers, the thunder among the clouds . .

Now that the laughter, broken in two, hangs tremulous between the
   teeth,
Remember, O dancers, the lightning beyond the earth . . .

The smell of blood already floats in the lavender-mist of the
   afternoon.
The death sentence lies in ambush along the corridors of power;
And a great fearful thing already tugs at the cables of the open air,
A nebula immense and immeasurable, a night of deep waters –
An iron dream unnamed and unprintable, a path of stone.

The drowsy heads of the pods in barren farmlands witness it,
The homesteads abandoned in this century's brush fire witness it:
The myriad eyes of deserted corn cobs in burning barns witness it:
Magic birds with the miracle of lightning flash on their feathers . . .

The arrows of God tremble at the gates of light,
The drums of curfew pander to a dance of death;

And the secret thing in its heaving
Threatens with iron mask
The last lighted torch of the century . . .

Wole Soyinka

Telephone Conversation

The price seemed reasonable, location
Indifferent. The landlady swore she lived
Off premises. Nothing remained
But self-confession. 'Madam,' I warned,
'I hate a wasted journey – I am African.'
Silence. Silenced transmission of
Pressurized good-breeding. Voice, when it came,
Lipstick coated, long gold-rolled
Cigarette-holder pipped. Caught I was, foully.
'HOW DARK?' . . . I had not misheard. . . . 'ARE YOU LIGHT
OR VERY DARK?' Button B. Button A. Stench
Of rancid breath of public hide-and-speak.
Red booth. Red pillar-box. Red double-tiered
Omnibus squelching tar. It *was* real! Shamed
By ill-mannered silence, surrender
Pushed dumbfoundment to beg simplification.
Considerate she was, varying the emphasis –
'ARE YOU DARK? OR VERY LIGHT?' Revelation came.
'You mean – like plain or milk chocolate?'
Her assent was clinical, crushing in its light
Impersonality. Rapidly, wave-length adjusted,
I chose. 'West African sepia' – and as afterthought,
'Down in my passport.' Silence for spectroscopic
Flight of fancy, till truthfulness clanged her accent
Hard on the mouthpiece. 'WHAT'S THAT?' conceding
'DON'T KNOW WHAT THAT IS.' 'Like brunette.'
'THAT'S DARK, ISN'T IT?' 'Not altogether.
Facially, I am brunette, but madam, you should see
The rest of me. Palm of my hand, soles of my feet
Are a peroxide blonde. Friction, caused –
Foolishly madam – by sitting down, has turned
My bottom raven black – One moment madam!' – sensing
Her receiver rearing on the thunderclap
About my ears – 'Madam,' I pleaded, 'wouldn't you rather
See for yourself?'

Seven poems from *Idanre & Other Poems* (1967)

Death in the Dawn

Traveller, you must set out
At dawn. And wipe your feet upon
The dog-nose wetness of the earth.

Let sunrise quench your lamps. And watch
Faint brush pricklings in the sky light
Cottoned feet to break the early earthworm
On the hoe. Now shadows stretch with sap
Not twilight's death and sad prostration.
This soft kindling, soft receding breeds
Racing joys and apprehensions for
A naked day. Burdened hulks retract,
Stoop to the mist in faceless throng
To wake the silent markets – swift, mute
Processions on grey byways. . . . On this
Counterpane, it was –
Sudden winter at the death
Of dawn's lone trumpeter. Cascades
Of white feather-flakes . . . but it proved
A futile rite. Propitiation sped
Grimly on, before.
The right foot for joy, the left, dread
And the mother prayed, Child
May you never walk
When the road waits, famished.

Traveller, you must set forth
At dawn.
I promise marvels of the holy hour
Presages as the white cock's flapped
Perverse impalement – as who would dare
The wrathful wings of man's Progression. . . .

But such another wraith! Brother,
Silenced in the startled hug of
Your invention – is this mocked grimace
This closed contortion – I?

Massacre, October '66

Written in Tegel

Shards of sunlight touch me here
Shredded in willows. Through stained-glass
Fragments on the lake I sought to reach
A mind at silt-bed

The lake stayed cold
I swam in an October flush of dying leaves
The gardener's labour flew in seasoned scrolls
Lettering the wind

Swept from painted craft
A mockery of waves remarked this idyll sham
I trod on acorns; each shell's detonation
Aped the skull's uniqueness.

Came sharper reckoning –
This favoured food of hogs cannot number high
As heads still harshly crop to whirlwinds
I have briefly fled

The oak rains a hundred more
A kind confusion to arithmetics of death:
Time to watch autumn the removal man
Dust down rare canvases

To let a loud resolve of passion
Fly to a squirrel, burnished light and copper fur
A distant stance without the lake's churchwindows
And for a stranger, love.

A host of acorns fell, silent
As they are silenced all, whose laughter
Rose from such indifferent paths, oh God
They are not strangers all

Whose desecration mocks the word
Of peace – *salaam aleikun* – not strangers any
Brain of thousands pressed asleep to pig fodder –
Shun pork the unholy – cries the priest.

I borrow seasons of an alien land
In brotherhood of ill, pride of race around me
Strewn in sunlit shards. I borrow alien lands
To stay the season of a mind.

Civilian and Soldier

My apparition rose from the fall of lead,
Declared, 'I'm a civilian.' It only served
To aggravate your fright. For how could I
Have risen, a being of this world, in that hour
Of impartial death! And I thought also: nor is
Your quarrel of this world.

                     You stood still
For both eternities, and oh I heard the lesson
Of your training sessions, cautioning –
Scorch earth behind you, do not leave
A dubious neutral to the rear. Reiteration
Of my civilian quandary, burrowing earth
From the lead festival of your more eager friends
Worked the worse on your confusion, and when
You brought the gun to bear on me, and death
Twitched me gently in the eye, your plight
And all of you came clear to me.

                     I hope some day
Intent upon my trade of living, to be checked
In stride by *your* apparition in a trench,
Signalling, I am a soldier. No hesitation then
But I shall shoot you clean and fair
With meat and bread, a gourd of wine
A bunch of breasts from either arm, and that
Lone question – do you friend, even now, know
What it is all about?

Prisoner

Grey, to the low grass cropping
Slung, wet-lichened, wisps from such
Smoke heaviness, elusive of thin blades
Curl inward to the earth, breed
The grey hours,
And days, and years, for do not
The wise grey temples we must build
To febrile years, here begin, not
In tears and ashes, but on the sad mocking
Threads, compulsive of the hour?

In the desert wildness, when, lone cactus,
Cannibal was his love – even amidst the
Crag and gorge, the leap and night-tremors
Even as the potsherd stayed and the sandstorm
Fell – intimations came.

In the whorled centre of the storm, a threnody
But not from this. For that far companion,
Made sudden stranger when the wind slacked
And the centre fell, grief. And the stricken
Potsherd lay, disconsolate – intimations then

But not from these. He knew only
Sudden seizure. And time conquest
Bound him helpless to each grey essence.

Nothing remained if pains and longings
Once, once set the walls. Sadness
Closed him, rootless, lacking cause.

Season

Rust is ripeness, rust
And the wilted corn-plume;
Pollen is mating-time when swallows
Weave a dance
Of feathered arrows
Thread corn-stalks in winged
Streaks of light. And, we loved to hear
Spliced phrases of the wind, to hear
Rasps in the field, where corn leaves
Pierce like bamboo slivers.

Now, garnerers we,
Awaiting rust on tassels, draw
Long shadows from the dusk, wreathe
Dry thatch in woodsmoke. Laden stalks
Ride the germ's decay – we await
The promise of the rust.

Night

Your hand is heavy, Night, upon my brow,
I bear no heart mercuric like the clouds, to dare
Exacerbation from your subtle plough.

Woman as a clam, on the sea's crescent
I saw your jealous eye quench the sea's
Fluorescence, dance on the pulse incessant

Of the waves. And I stood, drained
Submitting like the sands, blood and brine
Coursing to the roots. Night, you rained

Serrated shadows through dank leaves
Till, bathed in warm suffusion of your dappled cells
Sensations pained me, faceless, silent as night thieves.

Hide me now, when night children haunt the earth
I must hear none! These misted calls will yet
Undo me; naked, unbidden, at Night's muted birth.

Abiku*

In vain your bangles cast
Charmed circles at my feet
I am Abiku, calling for the first
And the repeated time.

Must I weep for goats and cowries
For palm oil and the sprinkled ash?
Yams do not sprout in amulets
To earth Abiku's limbs.

So when the snail is burnt in his shell,
Whet the heated fragment, brand me
Deeply on the breast. You must know him
When Abiku calls again.

I am the squirrel teeth, cracked
The riddle of the palm. Remember
This, and dig me deeper still into
The god's swollen foot.

Once and the repeated time, ageless
Though I puke; and when you pour
Libations, each finger points me near
The way I came, where

The ground is wet with mourning
White dew suckles flesh-birds
Evening befriends the spider, trapping
Flies in wind-froth;

Night, and Abiku sucks the oil
From lamps. Mothers! I'll be the
Supplicant snake coiled on the doorstep
Yours the killing cry.

The ripest fruit was saddest;
Where I crept, the warmth was cloying.
In the silence of webs, Abiku moans, shaping
Mounds from the yolk.

* Abiku: a 'spirit child'; one fated to a cycle of early death and rebirth to the same mother.

Two poems from *A Shuttle in the Crypt* (1972)

Ujamaa
(*for Julius Nyerere*)

Sweat is leaven for the earth
Not tribute. Earth replete
Seeks no homage from the toil of earth.
Sweat is leaven for the earth
Not driven homage to a fortressed god.
Your black earth hands unchain
Hope from death messengers, from
In-bred dogmanoids that prove
Grimmer than the Grim Reaper, insatiate
Predators on humanity, their fodder.
Sweat is leaven, bread, Ujamaa
Bread of the earth, by the earth
For the earth. Earth is all people.

Bearings III: Amber Wall

Breath of the sun, crowned
In green crepes and amber beads
Children's voices at the door of Orient

Raising eyelids on the sluggish earth
Dispersing sulphur fumes above the lake
Of awakening, you come hunting with the sun

His hands upon the loftiest branches
Halted on the prize, eyes in wonderlust
Questioned this mystery of man's isolation

Fantasies richer than burning mangoes
Flickered through his royal mind, an open
Noon above the door that closed

I would you may discover, mid-morning
To the man's estate, with lesser pain
The wall of gain within the outer loss

Your flutes at evening, your seed-awakening
Dances fill the night with growth; I hear
The sun's sad chorus to your starlit songs

John Pepper Clark

Seven poems from *A Reed in the Tide* (1965)

Olokun*

I love to pass my fingers,
As tide through weeds of the sea
And wind the tall fern-fronds
Through the strands of your hair
Dark as night that screens the naked moon:

I am jealous and passionate
Like Jehovah, God of the Jews,
And I would that you realize
No greater love had woman
From man than the one I have for you!

But what wakeful eyes of man,
Made of the mud of this earth,
Can stare at the touch of sleep
The sable vehicle of dream
Which indeed is the look of your eyes?

So drunken, like ancient walls
We crumble in heaps at your feet;
And as the good maid of the sea,
Full of rich bounties for men,
You lift us all beggars to your breast.

* Olokun: goddess of the sea.

Night Rain

What time of night it is
I do not know
Except that like some fish
Doped out of the deep
I have bobbed up bellywise
From stream of sleep
And no cocks crow.
It is drumming hard here
And I suppose everywhere
Droning with insistent ardour upon
Our roof-thatch and shed
And through sheaves slit open
To lightning and rafters
I cannot make out overhead
Great water drops are dribbling
Falling like orange or mango
Fruits showered forth in the wind
Or perhaps I should say so
Much like beads I could in prayer tell
Them on string as they break
In wooden bowls and earthenware
Mother is busy now deploying
About our roomlet and floor.
Although it is so dark
I know her practised step as
She moves her bins, bags, and vats
Out of the run of water
That like ants filing out of the wood
Will scatter and gain possession
Of the floor. Do not tremble then
But turn brothers, turn upon your side
Of the loosening mats
To where the others lie.
We have drunk tonight of a spell
Deeper than the owl's or bat's
That wet of wings may not fly.
Bedraggled upon the *iroko*, they stand
Emptied of hearts, and
Therefore will not stir, no, not

Even at dawn for then
They must scurry in to hide.
So we'll roll over on our back
And again roll to the beat
Of drumming all over the land
And under its ample soothing hand
Joined to that of the sea
We will settle to sleep of the innocent and free.

For Granny (from Hospital)

Tell me, before the ferryman's return,
What was that stirred within your soul,
One night fifteen floods today,
When upon a dugout
Mid pilgrim lettuce on the Niger,
You with a start strained me to breast:
Did you that night in the raucous voice
Of yesterday's rain,
Tumbling down banks of reed
To feed a needless stream,
Then recognize the loud note of quarrels
And endless dark nights of intrigue
In Father's house of many wives?
Or was it wonder at those footless stars
Who in their long translucent fall
Make shallow silten floors
Beyond the pale of muddy waters
Appear more plumbless than the skies?

197

Cry of Birth

An echo of childhood stalks before me
like evening shadows on the earth,
rolling back into piquant memory
the anguished cry of my birth;

Out of the caverns of nativity
a voice, I little knew as my own
and thought to have shed with infancy,
returns with a sharpness before unknown.

Poor castaways to this darkling shore,
void out of the sea of eternity
and blind, we catch by reflex horror
an instant glimpse, the guilt of our see:

The souls of men are steeped in stupor
who, tenants upon this wild isle unblest,
sleep on, oblivious of its loud nightmare
with wanton motions bedevilling our breast.

All night, through its long reaches and black
I wander as Io, driven by strange passions,
within and out, and for gadfly have at my back
one harrowing shriek of pain and factions –

It comes ceaseless as from the wilderness!
commingled with the vague cogitation
of the sea, its echo of despair and stress
precedes me like a shade to the horizon.

Abiku

Coming and going these several seasons,
Do stay out on the baobab tree,
Follow where you please your kindred spirits
If indoors it is not enough for you.
True, it leaks through the thatch
When floods brim the banks,
And the bats and the owls
Often tear in at night through the eaves,
And at harmattan, the bamboo walls
Are ready tinder for the fire
That dries the fresh fish up on the rack.
Still, it's been the healthy stock
To several fingers, to many more will be
Who reach to the sun.
No longer then bestride the threshold
But step in and stay
For good. We know the knife-scars
Serrating down your back and front
Like beak of the sword-fish,
And both your ears, notched
As a bondsman to this house,
Are all relics of your first comings.
Then step in, step in and stay
For her body is tired,
Tired, her milk going sour
Where many more mouths gladden the heart.

A Child Asleep

He who plucked light
From under shade of a tree
Sat so in dust, but in silence,
Passing like a spear clean into
The pith of things. But you,
Graft to an old bombax tree,
Raised on fulness of sap science
Cannot give, breed flies
In the oil of our evening,
Have sat dropsical feeding
On desire: it squashes, like dried
Out ribs of tobacco an old woman
Is turning into snuff you tried
To wreck with stones –
But oh look at what we spies
Have missed! In the sand
Here at our feet already fallen is
Your stool, and how clean
Past our fingers, teasing and
Tugging, you have slumped down
A natal stump, there shed
Distended in the dust – No!
As a primeval shadow
Tumbling head over heels into arms of light.

The Leader

They have felled him to the ground
Who announced home from abroad
Wrestled to a standstill his champion
Cousin the Killer of Cows. Yes,
In all that common
And swamp, pitched piecemeal by storks,
No iguana during a decade of tongues
Could throw or twist him round
While he rallied the race and clan.
Now like an alligator he lies
Trussed up in a house without eyes
And ears:
      Bit of bamboo,
Flung to laggard dogs by drowning
Nearest of kin, has quite locked his jaws.

From *Casualties* (1970)

Season of Omens

When calabashes held petrol and men
  turned faggots in the streets
Then came the five hunters
When mansions and limousines made
  bonfires in sunset cities
Then came the five hunters
When clans were discovered that were not in the book
  and cattle counted for heads of men
Then came the five hunters
When hoodlums took possession of police barracks
  in defiance of bullets
Then came the five hunters
When ministers legislated from bed and
  made high office the prize for failure
Then came the five hunters
When wads of notes were kept in infant skulls
  with full blessing of prelates
Then came the five hunters

When women grew heavy with ballot papers delivering
   the house entire to adulterers
Then came the five hunters
When a grand vizier in season of arson turned
   upon bandits in a far off place
Then came the five hunters
When men lost their teeth before they cut them
   to eat corn
Then came the five hunters
When a cabinet grew so broad the top gave way
   and trapped everyone therein
Then came the five hunters

At club closure,
Antelopes slept, for lions snored;
Then struck the five hunters,
But not together, not together.
One set out on his own into the night,
Four down their different spoors by the sea;
By light of stars at dawn
Each read in the plan a variant

And so one morning
The people woke up to a great smoke.
There was fire all right,
But who lighted it, where
The lighter of the fire?

Fallen in the grass was the lion,
Fallen in the forest was the jackal,
Missing by the sea was the shepherd-sheep,
His castrate ram in tow,
And all around was the blood of hounds.

Frank Aig-Imoukhuede

One Wife for One Man

I done try go church, I done go for court
Dem all day talk about di 'new culture':
Dem talk about 'equality', dem mention 'divorce'
Dem holler am so-tay my ear nearly cut;
     One wife be for one man.

My fader before my fader get him wife borku.*
E no' get equality palaver; he live well
For he be oga† for im own house.
But dat time done pass before white man come
Wit 'im
     One wife for one man,

Tell me how una‡ woman no go make yanga§
Wen'e know say na'im only dey.
Suppose say – make God no 'gree – 'e no born at all?§§
A'tell you dat man bin dey crazy wey start
     One wife for one man.

Jus' tell me how one wife fit do one man;
How go fit stay all time for him house
For time when belleh done kommot.
How many pickin', self, one woman fit born
     Wen one wife be for one man?

Suppose, self, say no so-so woman your wife dey born
Suppose your wife sabe book, no'sabe make chop;
Den, how you go tell man make'e no' go out
Sake of dis divorce? Bo, dis culture na waya O!
     Wen one wife be for one man.

---

* bokru = plenty. † oga = master or Lord. ‡ una = variation of 'your'.
§ yanga = vanity, pride, and perversity. §§ she has no children.

Okogbule Wonodi

Planting

Lights on the shore
that was our port,
that was our fort;

and wind swaying scenes
that we know
       aside,
while the sea shells
stand aside,
season aside to make
mouths at us

birds on the stems,
pecking at the scare-crows
to call the farmer home,
who then shall follow,
with white shirts
the dance of his father
as tractors bite down
the yam god
and the squirrels skip about
making faces at us?

Stand
You that hate not
and praise not
these shifting scenes,
season and blow
the horn of *Rebisi*;*
that we,
who shall hear
the cock at night
and see the red snake at day

* Rebisi: ancestral god of the Diobu people.

and they that shall follow,
bow not
when the sea shells
season aside
making mouths at us.

Salute to Icheke

When did I cease to be
the bird that I have been;
was it that I have fallen
sullen at midstream,
or immersed earthwise
I have gone dusty with wives
that cook for men with irregularities
between their thighs?

    No father.
I am yet your harp;
tune me but fingerly
and my strings will echo
songs of my inside.

I am your right hand,
I will mend your barn
and girdle my breath
for after this harvest
there's the visit adults
and orphans will call
from windowless houses;
then will come the test
of my planting songs.

Michael Echeruo

Melting Pot

It is dark, now, and grave

This bowl of a world
That rings me round and round
And will not let me marvel enough
At this dull sky
At the ignorance of these men
Who cannot know what chance can do

I shudder
Before this bowl of a world,
At this dull sky.

Will they not, all of them,
Call me names when they hear
Their blind man of this city
Stumbled on an udara underfoot
And lost it in the search for more?

Wish they could see half
What my eyes see, or know
Half what I know!
The Century's blind man!

Man and God Distinguished

Man sees the stars
  and turns aside
  suspicious of such tidings
  on a perilous midnight.

Man turns his face
  from the terrors of incense
  for the tigers are howling
  when Man means to go home
  on a star-spangled midnight.

There can be no salt, and no joy
  from fresh dew in the morning,
  from wife or from home or from life
  in the wake of such tidings
  as stars and terrors of incense.

Afterwards, Man dies.

Sheets with the whiteness of stars
  and incense and oil and dirt
  and tongue knowing no spices, no salt.

And the cold angel caresses the God!

Pol N Ndu

udude
(*at cock crow*)

grave number twenty-four
red axe forged from last burials
of twenty-three corpses in me:
Okpoko

horn-man call,
nude queens low in chant
far from lay-men
far from grasshoppers
trembling at your charged incantations:
Mmanwu

transmitting dead-land rumbles
in diction computed
at first cock-crow:
Udude

raw-material un-human
in invincible cocoon
explaining miracle photogropic:
burst-balloon

time-keeper of innumerable sperms
frantic in vibration
to chaotic chemistry:
I win!

The purest victory of all. . . .
victory of vision
        of visitation
        of creation
perfect without cohtribution,
new-born fire-intricate
delicate because sharp
fierce in steadiness

I yearn

Evacuation

Distance
explodes
with cannon

Fire flakes
rain with
fire balls

the shrieking
the sleeping
the naked
the ragged
the clothed

melting
in the frenzy

weird things
herding nowhere

reset
the tents
in sulphur
or in sun

Onwuchekwa Jemie

Iroko

1

Old chronicler
landscape mirror without a memory
whose annals are the cipher
      of blood and earth
      tangled in your veins
seeing and waiting and saying nothing
silent as the desert sand –
who can discover the secrets of the iroko
         on the village square?

See here
shortlegged generation
striding from peak to peak
      past present
      from past to future
stand a moment and contemplate the iroko
apotheosis of the tense present
waiting
waiting for its date with the bulldozer

2

Come, labyrinth
knowledge makes us unhappy
the iroko tells us nothing

Toward a Poetics

1

The great dark work
              has not yet been written
  a monument to our age
             which is the age of negritude

It will be written by a pop artist
  who will dismember his contemporaries
      image by image
            and phrase by phrase

and
    adding a touch of dung
             a dash of dirt and corn
      will reassemble them
             in a fierce startling
        collation

2

    To speak with a public voice
  the poet must be
             angry with the world
    and the way it is
             He must speak with rage
tempered by grandeur
      The sugarcandy school is not worth a line
        The prophets of doom offer nothing
            but unreal visions
      of strange places ruined
           empty cupolas
      void niches
            vacant dais
and under the arches dust and scorpions
  in the vaults spiders
               rats
      wind broken-broken
        From a gloomy corner
            angels cart off
               the coffin of God

But you who have known no God
but forests and waterfalls
and the bitter sun
you will articulate the totality
the embarrassment
pride
despair
and hope
and never forget the hope
of a continent in earthquake
You will speak
of black and white
and sometimes of red
trisyllabic reality
in which the earth is packed
awful tricolour
behind which the frightened spirit
hides itself
am reaching for
a modern grand style
to lift me away
words at a time
from the colourless
flat irony
of life

Aig Higo

Ritual Murder

No animals will live
Rivers will be dry
The rotund seal will snap
Eager vultures will show
The sacred spring is stained red with lust

Our seedlings bake on the rocks
Fresh leaves wither in pain
The black-robed virgins ate here, hot-eyed,
Breathing agony, prowling with parted lips.

I hear their voodoo dance to soothe
And melt the hurt strains of their trance.
They've come to mourn the spectral eunuchs of the shrine.

Hidesong

     I struck tomorrow square in the face
Yesterday groaned and said,
        'Please mind your steps today.'
    I left them swimming with today.

        Hidesong
        Birdsong
        Unto my soul
        What funeral pyre rejects your bones?

        My spider soul is spinning
        Spinning
          Spinning endlessly.

Scarabwise I tow my days along
Alone I tow my death along.

Molara Ogundipe-Leslie

Song at the African Middle Class
(for Augustinho Neto)

we charge through the skies of disillusion,
seeking the widening of eyes, we gaze at chaos,
speak to deadened hearts and ears stopped with
commerce. We drift around our region of clowns,
walking on air as dreams fly behind some eyes,
some forage among broken bodies, fractured minds
to find just ways retraced and new like beaten cloth.

and if they come again
will they come again?
and if they come again
will they dance this time?
will the new egunguns dance once more
resplendent in rich-glassed cloths?
will they be of their people's needs,
rise to those needs, settle whirling rifts
salve, O, festering hearts?
will they say when they come
O my people, O my people, how to love you delicately?

Niyi Osundare

The Sand Seer

Let your wandering fingers
Trek in these sands
And open up the vista
To the mystery of time.

You cast no nuts
Fling no cords
Ring no bells
Nor seek yesterlives
At the root of graveyard turf.

Vista atoms of practised
eyes, seen everywhere
Knowing the secret of
Every toe. Truths lie
Undressed and the riddle
of the marrow is cracked
Upon a grain of sooth.

Let the sparkle of these
Sands telescope enigmatic
Time and catch the bird on
Tomorrow's tree.

      which woman makes best wife
      which profession makes richest
      men, what to do or undo that
      I may live till I please?

The future shrinks to eye-shot
As you sit there counting
Lots in grains of sand.

I Sing of Change

Sing on: somewhere, at some new moon,
We'll learn that sleeping is not death,
Hearing the whole earth change its tune.
                                    W.B. Yeats.

I sing
of the beauty of Athens
without its slaves

Of a world free
of kings and queens
and other remnants
of an arbitrary past

Of earth
with no
sharp north
or deep south
without blind curtains
or iron walls

of the end
of warlords and armouries
and prisons of hate and fear

Of deserts treeing
and fruiting
after the quickening rains

Of the sun
radiating ignorance
and stars informing
nights of unknowing

I sing of a world reshaped

Odia Ofeimun

Let Them Choose Paths

They choose paths
who think there are paths to choose,
They make banners and float
our next republic.

They scour the garbage
of folklore
for the piece of silver
hidden by the wily tortoise.

They seek life
who cower at growths of lianas and creepers,
They run from the tangled stems
in search of stripped wisdom.

Pathfinders, all
they do not dare to know,
the thrill of building roads anew
too soft, too spiritless to stand
the course of sweat
down the smalls of their backs.

Let them choose paths
who think there are paths to choose.
We, we must grow new eyes
to see the asphalt in the chaste forest.

A Naming Day

Festive draperies override the claims of
bread and fresh air in this house

Gaudy buntings take breath away
from the newborn muffled in damask

in lace, in nameless riots of colours.
Mothers redress the loss of breast-milk

(so indecent to breast-feed children
now that mothers have turned mummies)

sorcerers of the supermarket conjuring
toys to people the lonesome hours
of unsung nurseries

Mothers have turned mummies
and growing up means to grind and wallow
in adult games of self-deceit
before the antimony of truth has time
to lay its fingers on the little heads

A Gong
(for Miriam Makeba)

Your voice awakens
the agony of brothers
drowned in their skokiaan tins
of pain

The naked virgin
from your limpid moon – out of
the dead sleep of children –
walks the thorned footpath
of my being

Is it all grief? –
this grey legend
of your night
gives birth to love, hope
gold landscapes
in tears and death

Is it mere sorcery? –
this rhythm swarms
with pagan tentacles upon moments
to baptize the world
with conscience, .
and unfurl an aura of innocence

Black woman, you rouse in me a bestial joy
whetting a desire to fight
to plunder, if only to fulfil
the promise,
the gentle gleam of that Canaan
on your horizons

Funso Aiyejina

Let Us Remember
(for Dax, a fellow traveller)

We who have listened to silences abort
before they were diagnosed
as stream-flow of seminal blood
out of tune with monthly cycles . . .

we who have collected clouds
that eventually burst into storms
and left us aghast as our crops
became feeders to ocean bound streams . . .

we who can point to fragments of kites
and strands of thread
entangled on high voltage cables
as evidence of our dispersed dreams . .

we who can smell the stench of dead pigeons
by the waterless fountains of our memorial squares
as evidence of the death of the *in*
in our independence . . .

we who have danced at festivals of arts
while cripples from new tribes
walk around on stilts and trample
our pre-harvest fields of crops to death . . .

let us remember
how men of parliament vacationed the electorate,
bandits demanded donations with which to refill
treasuries they had looted into family pots,
and power dissolved the people . . .

let us remember
how men, feline skunks, bury their insides sub rosa
forgetful of bamboo groves whose sacred flutes will grow
to play the tunes they plant into beachsand
and manifest the ugly lump on the king's crowned head
which he forbids his barber to proclaim before the people

May Ours Not Be

May ours not be like the story
of the Ear and the Mosquito;
but if it is, remember, o plunderers,
the Mosquito's eternal vow of protest,
for we shall become like lice
forever in your seams,
ant-heads that even in death
burrow deep into the flesh,
cameleon faeces that cannot
be wiped off the feet,
and regenerating earthworms
that multiply by their pieces;
if there is no rainbow in the sky,
we know to create one
by splashing water in the face of the sun;
if sleepers' hands protect their ears,
mosquitoes must learn to bite at their legs
to awaken them into their broken pledges;
if treasure hunters disturb our Orukwu rockhill,
thunder will break behind our tongues of lightning
like arrows in flight . . .

San Tomé

Aldo do Espirito Santo

Where Are the Men Seized in this Wind of Madness?

Blood falling in drops to the earth
men dying in the forest
and blood falling, falling . . .
on those cast into the sea. . . .
Fernão Dias for ever in the story
of Ilha Verde, red with blood,
of men struck down
in the vast arena of the quay.
Alas the quay, the blood, the men,
the fetters, the lash of beatings
resound, resound, resound
dropping in the silence of prostrated lives
of cries, and howls of pain
from men who are men no more,
in the hands of nameless butchers.
Zé Mulato in the story of the quay
shooting men in the silence
of bodies falling.
Alas Zé Mulato, Zé Mulato,
The victims cry for vengeance
The sea, the sea of Fernão Dias
devouring human lives
is bloody red.
– We are arisen –
Our eyes are turned to you.
Our lives entombed
in fields of death,
men of the Fifth of February
men fallen in the furnace of death
imploring pity
screaming for life,
dead without air, without water
they all arise

from the common grave
and upright in the chorus of justice
cry for vengeance....
   The fallen bodies in the forest,
the homes, the homes of men
destroyed in the gulf
of ravening fire,
lives incinerated,
raise the unaccustomed chorus of justice
crying for vengeance.
And all you hangmen
all you torturers
sitting in the dock:
– What have you done with my people? ...
– What do you answer?
– Where is my people? ...
And I answer in the silence
of voices raised
demanding justice....
One by one, through all the line....
For you, tormentors,
forgiveness has no name.
Justice shall be heard.
And the blood of lives fallen
in the forests of death,
innocent blood
drenching the earth
in a silence of terrors
shall make the earth fruitful,
crying for justice.
It is the flame of humanity
singing of hope
in a world without bonds
where liberty
is the fatherland of men....

Senegal

Léopold Sédar Senghor

In Memoriam

It is Sunday.
I fear the crowd of my brothers with stony faces.
From my tower of glass filled with pain, the nagging Ancestors
I gaze at roofs and hills in the fog
In the silence – the chimneys are grave and bare.
At their feet sleep my dead, all my dreams are dust
All my dreams, the liberal blood spills all along the streets, mixing
    with the blood of the butcheries.
And now, from this observatory as from a suburb
I watch my dreams float vaguely through the streets, lie at the hills'
    feet
Like the guides of my race on the banks of Gambia or Saloum.
Now of the Seine, at the feet of these hills.
Let me think of my dead!
Yesterday it was Toussaint, the solemn anniversary of the sun
And no remembrance in any cemetery.
Ah, dead ones who have always refused to die, who have known how
    to fight death
By Seine or Sine, and in my fragile veins pushed the invincible blood,
Protect my dreams as you have made your sons, wanderers on
    delicate feet.
Oh Dead, protect the roofs of Paris in the Sunday fog
The roofs which guard my dead
That from the perilous safety of my tower I may descend to the
    streets
To join my brothers with blue eyes
With hard hands.

Night of Sine

Woman, rest on my brow your balsam hands, your hands gentler than
   fur.
The tall palmtrees swinging in the nightwind
Hardly rustle. Not even cradlesongs,
The rhythmic silence rocks us.
Listen to its song, listen to the beating of our dark blood, listen
To the beating of the dark pulse of Africa in the mist of lost villages.
Now the tired moon sinks towards its bed of slack water,
Now the peals of laughter even fall asleep, and the bards themselves
Dandle their heads like children on the backs of their mothers.
Now the feet of the dancers grow heavy and heavy grows the tongue
   of the singers.
This is the hour of the stars and of the night that dreams
And reclines on this hill of clouds, draped in her long gown of milk.
The roofs of the houses gleam gently. What are they telling so
   confidently to the stars?
Inside the hearth is extinguished in the intimacy of bitter and sweet
   scents.
Woman, light the lamp of clear oil, and let the children in bed talk
   about their ancestors, like their parents.
Listen to the voice of the ancients of Elissa. Like we, exiled,
They did not want to die, lest their seminal flood be lost in the sand.
Let me listen in the smoky hut for the shadowy visit of propitious
   souls,
My head on your breast glowing, like a kuskus ball smoking out of
   the fire,
Let me breathe the smell of our dead, let me contemplate and repeat
   their living voice, let me learn
To live before I sink, deeper than the diver, into the lofty depth of
   sleep.

Luxembourg 1939

This morning at the Luxembourg, this autumn at the Luxembourg,
   as I lived and relived my youth

No loafers, no water, no boats upon the water, no children, no
   flowers.

Ah! the September flowers and the sunburnt cries of children who
   defied the coming winter.

Only two old boys trying to play tennis.

This autumn morning without children – the children's theatre is shut!

This Luxembourg where I cannot trace my youth, those years fresh as
   the lawns.

My dreams defeated, my comrades despairing, can it be so?

Behold them falling like leaves with the leaves, withered and
   wounded trampled to death the colour of blood

To be shovelled into what common grave?

I do not know this Luxembourg, these soldiers mounting guard.

They have put guns to protect the whispering retreat of Senators,

They have cut trenches under the bench where I first learnt the soft
   flowering of lips.

That notice again! Ah yes, dangerous youth!

I watch the leaves fall into the shelters, into the ditches, into the
   trenches

Where the blood of a generation flows.

Europe is burying the yeast of nations and the hope of newer races.

Blues

The spring has swept the ice from all my frozen rivers
My young sap trembles at the first caresses along the tender bark.
But see how in the midst of July I am blinder than the Arctic winter!
My wings beat and break against the barriers of heaven
No ray pierces the deaf vault of my bitterness.
What sign is there to find? What key to strike?
And how can god be reached by hurling javelins?
Royal Summer of the distant South, you will come too late,
    in a hateful September!
In what book can I find the thrill of your reverberation?
And on the pages of what book, on what impossible lips taste your
    delirious love?

The impatient fit leaves me. Oh! the dull beat of the rain on the
    leaves!
Just play me your 'Solitude', Duke, till I cry myself to sleep.

Prayer to Masks

Black mask, red mask, you black and white masks,
Rectangular masks through whom the spirit breathes,
I greet you in silence!
And you too, my lionheaded ancestor.
You guard this place, that is closed to any feminine laughter, to any
    mortal smile.
You purify the air of eternity, here where I breathe the air of my
    fathers.
Masks of markless faces, free from dimples and wrinkles,
You have composed this image, this my face that bends over the altar
    of white paper.
In the name of your image, listen to me!
Now while the Africa of despotism is dying – it is the agony of a
    pitiable princess
Like that of Europe to whom she is connected through the navel –
Now fix your immobile eyes upon your children who have been called
And who sacrifice their lives like the poor man his last garment
So that hereafter we may cry 'here' at the rebirth of the world being
    the leaven that the white flour needs.
For who else would teach rhythm to the world that has died of
    machines and cannons?
For who else should ejaculate the cry of joy, that arouses the dead
    and the wise in a new dawn?
Say, who else could return the memory of life to men with a torn
    hope?
They call us cotton heads, and coffee men, and oily men,
They call us men of death.
But we are the men of the dance whose feet only gain power when
    they beat the hard soil.

Visit

I dream in the intimate semi-darkness of an afternoon.
I am visited by the fatigues of the day,
The deceased of the year, the souvenirs of the decade,
Like the procession of the dead in the village on the horizon of the
    shallow sea.
It is the same sun bedewed with illusions,
The same sky unnerved by hidden presences,
The same sky feared by those who have a reckoning with the dead.
And suddenly my dead draw near to me. . . .

What Dark Tempestuous Night

What dark tempestuous night has been hiding your face?
And what claps of thunder frighten you from the bed
When the fragile walls of my breast tremble?
I shudder with cold, trapped in the dew of the clearing.
O, I am lost in the treacherous paths of the forest.
Are these creepers or snakes that entangle my feet?
I slip into the mudhole of fear and my cry is suffocated in a watery
    rattle.
But when shall I hear your voice again, happy luminous morn?
When shall I recognize myself again in the laughing mirror of eyes,
    that are large like windows?
And what sacrifice will pacify the white mask of the goddess?
Perhaps the blood of chickens or goats, or the worthless blood in my
    veins?
Or the prelude of my song, the ablution of my pride?

Give me propitious words.

New York
(*for jazz orchestra: trumpet solo*)

I

New York! At first I was confused by your beauty, by those great
    golden long-legged girls.
So shy at first before your blue metallic eyes, your frosted smile
So shy. And the anguish in the depths of skyscraper streets
Lifting eyes hawkhooded to the sun's eclipse.
Sulphurous your light and livid the towers with heads that thunderbolt
    the sky
The skyscrapers which defy the storms with muscles of steel and
    stone-glazed hide.
But two weeks on the bare sidewalks of Manhattan
– At the end of the third week the fever seizes you with the pounce of
    a leopard
Two weeks without rivers or fields, all the birds of the air
Falling sudden and dead on the high ashes of flat rooftops.
No smile of a child blooms, his hand refreshed in my hand,
No mother's breast, but only nylon legs. Legs and breasts that have
    no sweat nor smell.
No tender word for there are no lips, only artificial hearts paid for in
    hard cash
And no book where wisdom may be read. The painter's palette
    blossoms with crystals of coral.
Nights of insomnia oh nights of Manhattan! So agitated by flickering
    lights, while motor-horns howl of empty hours
And while dark waters carry away hygienic loves, like rivers flooded
    with the corpses of children.

2

Now is the time of signs and reckonings
New York! Now is the time of manna and hyssop.
You must but listen to the trombones of God, let your heart beat in
the rhythm of blood, your blood.
I saw in Harlem humming with noise with stately colours and
flamboyant smells
– It was teatime at the house of the seller of pharmaceutical products –
I saw them preparing the festival of night for escape from the day.
I proclaim night more truthful than the day.
It was the pure hour when in the streets God makes the life that goes
back beyond memory spring up
All the amphibious elements shining like suns.
Harlem Harlem! Now I saw Harlem! A green breeze of corn springs
up from the pavements ploughed by the naked feet of dancers
Bottoms waves of silk and sword-blade breasts, water-lily ballets and
fabulous masks.
At the feet of police-horses roll the mangoes of love from low houses.
And I saw along the sidewalks streams of white rum streams of black
milk in the blue fog of cigars.
I saw the sky in the evening snow cotton-flowers and seraphims' wings
and sorcerers' plumes.
Listen New York! Oh listen to your male voice of brass vibrating with
oboes, the anguish choked with tears falling in great clots of blood
Listen to the distant beating of your nocturnal heart, rhythm and
blood of the tom-tom, tom-tom blood and tom-tom.

3

New York! I say to you: New York let black blood flow into your
  blood
That it may rub the rust from your steel joints, like an oil of life,
That it may give to your bridges the bend of buttocks and the
  suppleness of creepers.
Now return the most ancient times, the unity recovered, the
  reconciliation of the Lion the Bull and the Tree
Thought linked to act, ear to heart, sign to sense.
There are your rivers murmuring with scented crocodiles and
  mirage-eyed manatees. And no need to invent the Sirens.
But it is enough to open the eyes to the rainbow of April
And the ears, above all the ears, to God who out of the laugh of a
  saxophone created the heaven and the earth in six days.
And the seventh day he slept the great sleep of the Negro.

You Held the Black Face
(*for Khalam*)

You held the black face of the warrior between your hands
Which seemed with fateful twilight luminous.
From the hill I watched the sunset in the bays of your eyes.
When shall I see my land again, the pure horizon of your face?
When shall I sit at the table of your dark breasts?
The nest of sweet decisions lies in the shade.
I shall see different skies and different eyes,
And shall drink from the sources of other lips, fresher than lemons,
I shall sleep under the roofs of other hair, protected from storms.
But every year, when the rum of spring kindles the veins afresh,
I shall mourn anew my home, and the rain of your eyes over the
  thirsty savannah.

I Will Pronounce Your Name
(for Tama)

I will pronounce your name, Naëtt, I will declaim you, Naëtt!
Naëtt, your name is mild like cinnamon, it is the fragrance in which
    the lemon grove sleeps,
Naëtt, your name is the sugared clarity of blooming coffee trees
And it resembles the savannah, that blossoms forth under the
    masculine ardour of the midday sun.
Name of dew, fresher than shadows of tamarind,
Fresher even than the short dusk, when the heat of the day is
    silenced.
Naëtt, that is the dry tornado, the hard clap of lightning
Naëtt, coin of gold, shining coal, you my night, my sun!..
I am your hero, and now I have become your sorcerer, in order to
    pronounce your names.
Princess of Elissa, banished from Futa on the fateful day.

Be Not Amazed

Be not amazed beloved, if sometimes my song grows dark,
If I exchange the lyrical reed for the Khalam or the tama
And the green scent of the ricefields, for the swiftly galloping war
    drums.
I hear the threats of ancient deities, the furious cannonade of the god.
Oh, tomorrow perhaps, the purple voice of your bard will be silent
    for ever.
That is why my rhythm becomes so fast, that the fingers bleed on the
    Khalam.
Perhaps, beloved, I shall fall tomorrow, on a restless earth
Lamenting your sinking eyes, and the dark tom-tom of the mortars
    below.
And you will weep in the twilight for the glowing voice that sang your
    black beauty.

Birago Diop

Diptych

The Sun hung by a thread
In the depths of the Calabash dyed indigo
Boils the great Pot of Day.
Fearful of the approach of the Daughters of fire
The Shadow squats at the feet of the faithful.
The savannah is bright and harsh
All is sharp, forms and colours.
But in the anguished Silences made by Rumours
Of tiny sounds, neither hollow nor shrill,
Rises a ponderous Mystery,
A Mystery muffled and formless
Which surrounds and terrifies us.

The dark Loincloth pierced with nails of fire
Spread out on the Earth covers the bed of Night.
Fearful at the approach of the Daughters of shadow
The dog howls, the horse neighs
The Man crouches deep in his house.
The savannah is dark,
All is black, forms and colours
And in the anguished Silences made by Rumours
Of tiny sounds infinite or hollow or sharp
The tangled Paths of the Mystery
Slowly reveal themselves
For those who set out
And for those who return.

Vanity

If we tell, gently, gently
All that we shall one day have to tell,
Who then will hear our voices without laughter,
Sad complaining voices of beggars
Who indeed will hear them without laughter?

If we cry roughly of our torments
Ever increasing from the start of things,
What eyes will watch our large mouths
Shaped by the laughter of big children
What eyes will watch our large mouths?

What heart will listen to our clamouring?
What ear to our pitiful anger
Which grows in us like a tumour
In the black depth of our plaintive throats?

When our Dead come with their Dead
When they have spoken to us with their clumsy voices;
Just as our ears were deaf
To their cries, to their wild appeals
Just as our ears were deaf
They have left on the earth their cries,
In the air, on the water, where they have traced their signs
For us, blind deaf and unworthy Sons
Who see nothing of what they have made
In the air, on the water, where they have traced their signs.

And since we did not understand our dead
Since we have never listened to their cries
If we weep, gently, gently
If we cry roughly of our torments
What heart will listen to our clamouring,
What ear to our sobbing hearts?

Ball

A scroll of blue, an exquisite thought
Moves upwards in a secret accord
And the gentle pink explosion the shade filters
Drowns a woman's perfume in a heavy regret.

The languorous lament of the saxophone
Counts a string of troubles and vague promises
And, jagged or monotonous, its raucous cry
Sometimes awakes a desire I had thought dead.

Stop jazz, you scan the sobs and tears
That jealous hearts keep only to themselves.
Stop your scrap-iron din. Your uproar
Seems like a huge complaint where consent is born.

Viaticum

In one of the three pots
the three pots to which on certain evenings
the happy souls return
the serene breath of the ancestors,
the ancestors who were men,
the forefathers who were wise,
Mother wetted three fingers,
three fingers of her left hand:
the thumb, the index and the next;
I too wetted three fingers,
three fingers of my right hand:
the thumb, the index and the next.

With her three fingers red with blood,
with dog's blood,
with bull's blood,
with goat's blood,
Mother touched me three times.
She touched my forehead with her thumb,
With her index my left breast
And my navel with her middle finger.
I too held my fingers red with blood,
with dog's blood,

with bull's blood,
with goat's blood.
I held my three fingers to the winds
to the winds of the North, to the winds of the Levant,
to the winds of the South, to the winds of the setting sun;
and I raised my three fingers towards the Moon,
towards the full Moon, the Moon full and naked
when she rested deep in the largest pot.
Afterwards I plunged my three fingers in the sand
in the sand that had grown cold.
Then Mother said, 'Go into the world, go!
They will follow your steps in life.'

Since then I go
I follow the pathways
the pathways and roads
beyond the sea and even farther,
beyond the sea and beyond the beyond;
And whenever I approach the wicked,
the Men with black hearts,
whenever I approach the envious,
the Men with black hearts
before me moves the Breath of the Ancestors.

David Diop

Listen Comrades

Listen comrades of the struggling centuries
To the keen clamour of the Negro from Africa to the Americas
They have killed Mamba
As they killed the seven of Martinsville
Or the Madagascan down there in the pale light on the prisons
He held in his look comrades
The warm faith of a heart without anguish
And his smile despite agony
Despite the wounds of his broken body
Kept the bright colours of a bouquet of hope
It is true that they have killed Mamba with his white hairs
Who ten times poured forth for us milk and light
I feel his mouth on my dreams
And the peaceful tremor of his breast
And I am lost again
Like a plant torn from the maternal bosom
But no
For there rings out higher than my sorrows
Purer than the morning where the wild beast wakes
The cry of a hundred people smashing their cells
And my blood long held in exile
The blood they hoped to snare in a circle of words
Rediscovers the fervour that scatters the mists
Listen comrades of the struggling centuries
To the keen clamour of the Negro from Africa to the Americas
It is the sign of the dawn
The sign of brotherhood which comes to nourish the dreams of men.

Your Presence

In your presence I rediscovered my name
My name that was hidden under the pain of separation
I rediscovered the eyes no longer veiled with fever
And your laughter like a flame piercing the shadows
Has revealed Africa to me beyond the snows of yesterday
Ten years my love
With days of illusions and shattered ideas
And sleep made restless with alcohol
The suffering that burdens today with the taste of tomorrow
And that turns love into a boundless river
In your presence I have rediscovered the memory of my blood
And necklaces of laughter hung around our days
Days sparkling with ever new joys.

The Renegade

My brother you flash your teeth in response to every hypocrisy
My brother with gold-rimmed glasses
You give your master a blue-eyed faithful look
My poor brother in immaculate evening dress
Screaming and whispering and pleading in the parlours of
    condescension
We pity you
Your country's burning sun is nothing but a shadow
On your serene 'civilized' brow
And the thought of your grandmother's hut
Brings blushes to your face that is bleached
By years of humiliation and bad conscience
And while you trample on the bitter red soil of Africa
Let these words of anguish keep time with your restless step –
Oh I am lonely so lonely here.

Africa

Africa my Africa
Africa of proud warriors in ancestral savannahs
Africa of whom my grandmother sings
On the banks of the distant river
I have never known you
But your blood flows in my veins
Your beautiful black blood that irrigates the fields
The blood of your sweat
The sweat of your work
The work of your slavery
The slavery of your children
Africa tell me Africa
Is this you this back that is bent
This back that breaks under the weight of humiliation
This back trembling with red scars
And saying yes to the whip under the midday sun
But a grave voice answers me
Impetuous son that tree young and strong
That tree there
In splendid loneliness amidst white and faded flowers
That is Africa your Africa
That grows again patiently obstinately
And its fruit gradually acquires
The bitter taste of liberty.

The Vultures

In those days
When civilization kicked us in the face
When holy water slapped our cringing brows
The vultures built in the shadow of their talons
The bloodstained monument of tutelage
In those days
There was painful laughter on the metallic hell of the roads
And the monotonous rhythm of the paternoster
Drowned the howling on the plantations
O the bitter memories of extorted kisses
Of promises broken at the point of a gun
Of foreigners who did not seem human
Who knew all the books but did not know love
But we whose hands fertilize the womb of the earth
In spite of your songs of pride
In spite of the desolate villages of torn Africa
Hope was preserved in us as in a fortress
And from the mines of Swaziland to the factories of Europe
Spring will be reborn under our bright steps.

Sierra Leone

Syl Cheney-Coker

Six poems from *The Graveyard also has Teeth* (1980)

On Being a Poet in Sierra Leone

A poet alone in my country
I am seeking the verisimilitudes in life
the fire of metaphors the venom of verse
my country you are my heart living like a devastated landscape
always the magic of being underground of burying truth
of shedding your metaphysical form
country I wish to die being your poet
I who have so condemned and sold you
I who have so loved and hated you
imagine my sadness, the poetry of being you
a colossus strangled by fratricidal parasites
have I betrayed you writing my hermetic poetry
I suffer the estrangement of being too 'intellectual'
at the university the professors talk about the poetry
of Syl Cheney-Coker condemning students
to read me in the English honours class
my country I do not want that!
do not want to be cloistered in books alone
I want to be the albatross learning and living your fits
I want only to plough your fields
to be the breakfast of the peasants who read
to help the fishermen bring in their catch
I want to be your national symbol of life
because my heart is heavy country and exile calls
beating the pangs of oblivion on my brow
I want once more like the common man
to love a woman without dying of love
to leave a son or daughter to remember my grave
country you my pain, my phoenix, my disastrous gloating python
in whose belly all my anger dies

I am going to be happy to stop carrying my pain
like a grenade in my heart, I want to be simple
if possible to live with you, and then one day die leaving
my poetry, an imperfect metaphor of life!

Poem for a Guerrilla Leader
(*to Amilcar Cabral*)

Solitude supporting solitude on two pergolas
sunset shaping summer where the jungle closes in
man eating roots leaning on the theories of Fanon
it was there in his shadow that I saw the primordium of Africa

slaves supporting treachery behind sweet fraternal looks
minions of the bourgeoisie mingled with serfs
I know it all in serpentine bliss
feeling the tongues of fire obfuscating my life
cheek to cheek with that man in his solitude
murdered in his finest hour
by fratricidal negroes, brothers of lust!

to speak of his name I shed my sorrow
near this sea tormenting my memory with the cargoes of black flesh
bought with what portuguese asientos
sacred to the delight of the pope?
Ah when the journey was long sweetening the pain
my destiny to be born a slave enriching these brothers
who eat the flesh of wild boars . . .
my sadness knows it all piercing my heart!

and now the defoliated island rises colourless
the grass is the hands of those maimed by napalm
man-child leaping over the mutilated soul shouting
mother I am going away to be a revolutionary
to remake my brother I heard saying
O island O field you Cape Verde daughter in spoilage.

The Hunger of the Suffering Man

Sweating between his fingers, the agricultural man
sweating in his thorax the musician
sweating in his lungs the miner
sweating in his nausea the existential man
sweating in his refugee camp the Palestinian
driven out by the Jew who has forgotten Auschwitz
sweating in his ghetto the blackman
sweating in his carapace the animal-man
sweating when he escapes the innocent man
sweating in their duodena the children
battling the pigs on the garbage dump
sweating the woman whose urgent sex
brings me my brief joy
sweating the poor man whose house starves between the thighs
sweating the deadman, the marginal man
who wants his bones enamelled in gold
sweating the poor who died from the too, too rich
sweating the bronze man who suffers them all
sweating I who sing them!

SIERRA LEONE

Poem for a Lost Lover
(*to Merle Alexander*)

Eyes of heavenly essence, O breasts of the purity of breasts
Russian sapphire of the blue of eyes
O wine that mellows like the plenitude of Bach
Sargassian sea that is the calm of your heart
the patience of you loving my fragile soul
the courage of you moulding my moody words
I love you woman gentle in my memory!

O woman of the thirst of Siddhartha's love
you that I lost in the opium of my youth
have you fallen among the rocks off the New England coast
or now in premature grey nurse a stubborn tear
at the window watching winter's snow-coated leaves
here the tropical blossom of an African November
breathes gently on the tree of my heart
Oh that you could have known it woman of the sexual waters
heart of the spirit born of that love
dressing continents with garlands for whom I say
night strike my heart with the purest verse!

252

Letter to a Tormented Playwright
(*for Yulisa Amadu Maddy*)

Amadu I live alone inside four walls of books
some I have read others will grow cobwebs
or maybe like some old friends and lovers
will fade away with their undiscovered logic

the world that I have seen: New York
where I suffered the suicidal brother
and London where I discovered Hinostroza
Delgado, Ortega, Heraud and the other
Andean poets with a rage very much like ours!

remember Amadu how terrible I said it was
that you were in exile and working
in the Telephone Office in touch with all
the languages of the world but with no world
to call your own; how sad you looked that winter
drinking your life and reading poetry with me
in the damp chilly English coffee shops

                    *

remember I said how furious I was
that Vallejo had starved to death in Paris
that Rabéarivelo had killed himself
suffocated by an imaginary France
and I introduced Neruda and Guillen to you
and how in desperation we sought solace in the house
of John La Rose, that courageous Trinidadian poet

Amadu I am writing to you from the dungeon of my heart
the night brings me my grief and I am passive
waiting for someone to come, a woman
a friend, someone to soothe my dying heart!

now the memory of our lives brings a knife to my poems
our deaths which so burdened the beautiful Martiniquan
you said made you happy, she made you so happy, you a tormented
    playwright

                    *

253

sadness returns, the apparitions of my brothers
and my mother grows old thinking about them
and also seeing so much sadness in me her living and dying son
my mother who wishes me happy, who wants me to relive the son
she lost to poetry like a husband a wife to a trusted friend

but already the walls are closing around me
the rain has stopped and once again I am alone
waiting for them, the politicians of our country to come for me
to silence my right to shouting poetry loud in the parks
but who can shut up the rage the melodrama of being Sierra Leone
the farce of seeing their pictures daily in the papers
the knowledge of how though blindfolded and muzzled
something is growing, bloating, voluptuous and not despairing
I say to you for now, I embrace you brother.

The Road to Exile Thinking of Vallejo

Like others I get drunk in my blood
hiccuping and await the souls of my brothers
perennially on the song composed by the heliotrope heart
at midstream where the spirits walk
undisturbed!
excellent then, this sudden shower of locusts
expanse of cortege and the two roads
of the cemetery where time has its teeth
in the flesh of a mother who oxidizes her soul
with the waters of the passion-flower
as May is a brother just as October was a brother
linked to the prodigal who declares:

Mother I want to return into exile to be your poet!

hearing this, my mother seized by an element of nature
wondering whether I am going or staying seeing the roads
in my eyes, turns a terra-cotta sister and her hair
once black illuminates the night with its premature whiteness

my mother prevents my flight into myself
speaking to me through her silence through the beat of her heart
being that she loves me that she is always herself double
the sword fighting my days the lamp lighting my nights
when my heart sinks deep in the oasis
of its pain! she rejuvenates me calling back the me
that has died tracing the man-child to the poet
without understanding the dictates of my soul

*

blood absent from my soul my dog-starved days
on the peninsula of my Sierra Leone
my legacies which I counted in five carcasses
dancing drunk in the terrible summers
and that cruel winter polyphonic in verse

when I loved that woman without first learning how to live
I bled one night shedding poems from my heart!

It is recorded then: I'll die in exile!
thinking of my Sierra Leone
this country which has made me a poet
this country which has honoured me
with the two knives of my death passed crisscross
through my heart
so that I can say to a bleeding mother:

Mother I am returning into exile to be your poet!

From *The Blood in the Desert's Eyes*

The Philosopher

Who lived here when the stones were green
verdigris of age when the reptilians marched like men
into the night before that morning the sea
emptying its cup of wounds like a chasm of revolt.
like a castaway an old man kept his books in a cave
desolate his memory of life a portrait
like an abstraction of years, he lived
forgotten by others before the last tidal wave
1 consecrate him seer his beard was a white book
where we read about kings and prophets
planners of the ruins astride our stormy conscience
to write what history the moon already dripping its sea of red blood

the whirlwind that licked over your body
amulet of season playing fangs on the translucent word
flagellant at crossroads where the word was nailed
neologist who dressed the world in hendecasyllabic verse
O monk saddened when you consecrated the word in body
stripped when you meditated in penury

you return shadow from shadow the word
transformed into phoenix you return the man
reigning the length of the raised cross
violated your soul we fashion you into memory
drift of a cyclone, man with whom we raise our conscience
you rise from your body to be equal to your name!

South Africa

Dennis Brutus

At a Funeral

(for Valencia Majombozi, who died shortly after qualifying as a doctor.)

Black, green and gold at sunset: pageantry
And stubbled graves Expectant, of eternity,
In bride's-white, nun's-white veils the nurses gush their bounty
Of red-wine cloaks, frothing the bugled dirging slopes
Salute! Then ponder all this hollow panoply
For one whose gifts the mud devours, with our hopes.

Oh all you frustrate ones, powers tombed in dirt,
Aborted, not by Death but carrion books of birth
Arise! The brassy shout of Freedom stirs our earth;
Not Death but death's-head tyranny scythes our ground
And plots our narrow cells of pain defeat and dearth:
Better that we should die, than that we should lie down.

Nightsong: City

Sleep well, my love, sleep well:
the harbour lights glaze over restless docks,
police cars cockroach through the tunnel streets

from the shanties creaking iron-sheets
violence like a bug-infested rag is tossed
and fear is immanent as sound in the wind-swung bell;

the long day's anger pants from sand and rocks;
but for this breathing night at least,
my land, my love, sleep well.

This Sun on this Rubble

This sun on this rubble after rain.

Bruised though we must be
some easement we require
unarguably, though we argue against desire.

Under jackboots our bones and spirits crunch
forced into sweat-tear-sodden slush
– now glow-lipped by this sudden touch:

– sun-stripped perhaps, our bones may later sing
or spell out some malignant nemesis
Sharpevilled to spearpoints for revenging

but now our pride-dumbed mouths are wide
in wordless supplication
– are grateful for the least relief from pain

– like this sun on this debris after rain.

Poems About Prison

1

Cold

the clammy cement
sucks our naked feet

a rheumy yellow bulb
lights a damp grey wall

the stubbled grass
wet with three o'clock dew
is black with glittery edges;

we sit on the concrete,
stuff with our fingers
the sugarless pap
into our mouths

then labour erect;

form lines;

steel ourselves into fortitude
or accept an image of ourselves
numb with resigned acceptance;

the grizzled senior warder comments:
'Things like these
I have no time for;

they are worse than rats;
you can only shoot them.'

Overhead
the large frosty glitter of the stars
the Southern Cross flowering low;

the chains on our ankles
and wrists
that pair us together
jangle

glitter.

We begin to move
        awkwardly.

(*Colesberg: en route to Robben Island*)

Mazisi Kunene

The Echoes

Over the vast summer hills
I shall commission the maternal sun
To fetch you with her long tilted rays,

The slow heave of the valleys
Will once again roll the hymns of accompaniment
Scattering the glitter of the milky way over the bare fields.

You will meet me
Underneath the shadow of the timeless earth
Where I lie weaving the seasons.

You will indulge in the sway dances of your kin
To the time of symphonic flutes
Ravishing the identity of water lilies.

I have opened the mountain gates
So that the imposing rim
Of the Ruwenzori shall steal your image.

Even the bubbling lips of continents
(To the shy palms of Libya)
Shall awake the long-forgotten age.

The quivering waters of the Zambezi river
Will bear on a silvery blanket your name
Leading it to the echoing of the sea.

Let me not love you alone
Lest the essence of your being
Lie heavy on my tongue
When you count so many to praise.

Elegy

O Mzingeli son of the illustrious clans
You whose beauty spreads across the Tukela estuary
Your memory haunts like two eagles
We have come to the ceremonial ruins
We come to mourn the bleeding sun
We are the children of Ndungunya of the Dlamini clan
They whose grief strikes fear over the earth
We carry the long mirrors in the afternoon
Recasting time's play past infinite night.

O great departed ancestors
You promised us immortal life with immortal joys
But how you deceived us!

We invited the ugly salamander
To keep watch over a thousand years with a thousand sorrows
She watched to the far end of the sky
Sometimes terrorized by the feet of departed men
One day the furious storms
One day from the dark cyclone
One day in the afternoon
We gazed into a barren desert
Listening to the tremendous voices in the horizon
And loved again in the epics
And loved incestuous love!

We count a million
Strewn in the dust of ruined capitals
The bull tramples us on an anthill
We are late in our birth
Accumulating violent voices
Made from the lion's death
You whose love comes from the stars
Have mercy on us!
Give us the crown of thunder
That our grief may overhang the earth

O we are naked at the great streams
Wanderers greet us no more . . .

Thought on June 26

Was I wrong when I thought
All shall be avenged?
Was I wrong when I thought
The rope of iron holding the neck of young bulls
Shall be avenged?
Was I wrong
When I thought the orphans of sulphur
Shall rise from the ocean?
Was I depraved when I thought there need not be love,
There need not be forgiveness, there need not be progress,
There need not be goodness on the earth,
There need not be towns of skeletons,
Sending messages of elephants to the moon?
Was I wrong to laugh asphyxiated ecstasy
When the sea rose like quicklime
When the ashes on ashes were blown by the wind
When the infant sword was left alone on the hill top?
Was I wrong to erect monuments of blood?
Was I wrong to avenge the pillage of Caesar?
Was I wrong? Was I wrong?
Was I wrong to ignite the earth
And dance above the stars
Watching Europe burn with its civilization of fire,
Watching America disintegrate with its gods of steel,
Watching the persecutors of mankind turn into dust
Was I wrong? Was I wrong?

Sipho Sepamla

On Judgement Day

> black people are born singers
> black people are born runners
> black people are peace-loving
these myths make of us naïvete

we have been sipped with bubbles of champagne
we have known choking dust
and have writhed with the pain of humiliation

> singers
> runners
> peace-loving

nobody really sees the storm raging within us
nobody cares to know that we've reached our own bottom

laughing has become agonizing

> singers
> runners
> peace-loving
>   my foot

I fear we will all sing at night-vigils
and as I see things we will all run for cover
what I don't know is which peace will still be lovable

Civilization Aha

i thought of eden
                    the first time i ate a fig
i thought of a whiteman
                            the first time i saw god's
                                        portrait
i thought of a blackman
                            the first time i met satan on
                                        earth
i must be honest
                it wasn't only bantu education
            it was all part of what they say is western
                                    civilization

Talk to the Peach Tree

Let's talk to the swallows visiting us in summer
ask how it is in other countries

Let's talk to the afternoon shadow
ask how the day has been so far

Let's raise our pets to our level
ask them what they don't know of us

        words have lost meaning
        like all notations they've been misused

        most people will admit
        a whining woman can overstate her case

Talk to the paralysing heat in the air
inquire how long the mercilessness will last

Let's pick out items from the rubbish heap
ask how the stench is like down there

Let's talk to the peach tree
find out how it feels to be in the ground

Let's talk to the moon going down
ask if it isn't enough eyeing what's been going on

        come on
        let's talk to the devil himself
        it's about time

Keorapetse Kgositsile

The Air I Hear

The air, I hear,
froze to the sound
searching. And my memory
present and future tickles
the womb like the pulse
of this naked air
in the eye of a tear
drop. The dead cannot
remember even the memory
of death's laughter. But memory
defiant like the sound of pain
rides the wave at dawn
in the marrow of the desert
palm: stands looking still
and the bitter shape
of yesterdays weaves
timeless tomorrows
in the leaves
of laughter larger than
singular birth . . .

Song for Ilva Mackay and Mongane

Hear now a sound of floods
Of desire of longing of memories
Of erstwhile peasants who can
No longer laugh downhill. My brother
Knows there is no death in life
Only in death. That music is native
So I sing your name

You are child of your tongue
You will be born with gun
In one eye and grenade in the other
You are Tito: There is no such thing
As escape or sanctuary in life where
All things come to pass when they do
Where every bloodstain is a sign of death or life

You are Mandela You are all
The names we are in Robben Island
You are child of sound and sense
You can look the past
Straight in the eye
To know this season and purpose
You have come from yesterday
To remind the living that
The dead do not remember the banned
The jailed the exiled the dead
Here I meet you
And this way I salute you
With bloodstains on my tongue:

I am no calypsonian
But this you have taught me:
You could say you were from Capetown
Or Johannesburg Accra or Bagamoy
Newyork Kingston or Havana
When you have come from tomorrow
We shall know each other by our bloodstains

The Present is a Dangerous Place to Live

I In the Mourning

And at the door of the eye
is the still voice of the land.
My father before my father
knew the uses of fire
My father before my father,
with his multiple godhead,
sat on his circular stool
after the day was done. At times even
between the rednesses of two suns,
knowing that time was not born yesterday.
The circle continues
Time will always be
in spite of minutes that know no life.
Lives change in life
At times even rot
or be trampled underfoot
as the back of a slave.
There are cycles in the circle
I may even moan my deadness
or mourn your death,
in this sterile moment asking:
Where is the life we came to live?
Time will always be
Pastpresentfuture is always now
Where then is the life we came to live?

IV Mirrors, Without Song

Do not tell me, my brother, to reach
out and touch my soul. My soul is
inside and thin
and knows your death too

Does it matter then how
often my teeth are seen
when I laugh less and less?

Morning does not wake up
with my eye out the window
moaning, or mourning,
a thing or day gone to waste

I die in the world
and live my deadness
in my head, laughing
less and less.

Do you see now
another day, like a slave,
shows its face to be nothing,
nothing but a mirror of the death of another?

When I laugh, my brother, less and less
do not tell me to reach
out and touch my soul. My
soul is inside and thin
and knows your death too.

Oswald Mtshali

Inside My Zulu Hut

It is a hive
without any bees
to build the walls
with golden bricks of honey.
A cave cluttered
with a millstone,
calabashes of sour milk
claypots of foaming beer
sleeping grass mats
wooden head rests
tanned goat skins
tied with riempies
to wattle rafters
blackened by the smoke
of kneaded cow dung
burning under
the three-legged pot
on the earthen floor
to cook my porridge.

Ride upon the Death Chariot

They rode upon
the death chariot
to their Golgotha –
three vagrants
whose papers to be in Caesar's empire
were not in order.

The sun
shrivelled their bodies
in the mobile tomb
as airtight as canned fish.

We're hot!
We're thirsty!
We're hungry!

The centurion
touched their tongues
with the tip
of a lance
dipped in apathy:

'Don't cry to me
but to Caesar who
crucifies you.'

A woman came
to wipe their faces.
She carried a dishcloth
full of bread and tea.

We're dying!

The centurion
washed his hands.

The Birth of Shaka

His baby cry
was of a cub
tearing the neck
of the lioness
because he was fatherless.

The gods
boiled his blood
in a clay pot of passion
to course in his veins.

His heart was shaped into an ox shield
to foil every foe.

Ancestors forged
his muscles into
thongs as tough
as wattle bark
and nerves
as sharp as
syringa thorns.

His eyes were lanterns
that shone from the dark valleys of Zululand
to see white swallows
coming across the sea.
His cry to two assassin brothers:

'Lo! you can kill me
but you'll never rule this land!'

Arthur Nortje

Up Late

Night here, the owners asleep upstairs:
the room's eyes shut, its voices dead,
though I admire it when its mirrors
oblige me with my presence. Looking ahead
needs glancing back to what I once
was, the time that mischance
borrowed my body to break it by terror.

Now the cameras rest in their elegant
leather coffins, having caught
the whirl of streets before the wheels go silent.
Rain trickles as the red biro writes my heart:
time demands no attention of the will,
the clock is yellow with black numerals.
The icebox resumes its purring descant.

This picture opens on the past. I rise
to study a calendar scene from what was home:
an old white mill, sentimental, South African Airways
(the blue lithe buck), peaceful, implausible. Some
fugitive sense holds back the bruising wave:
that gift to spend, my song where I arrive,
didn't I take it from the first dispiriting wilderness?

My mind burned and I shackled it
with squalid love, the violence of the flesh.
The quiet scars over my veins bit
less deep now than the knife or lash
could feel content about:
no longer need I shout
freedom in the house. I sit in light

here, the refugee's privilege. Nor do I want
fruit in a bowl, banana pleasure, the skin
that slides from my fingers, spent
because the soft heart only must be eaten.
Give me the whole experience to savour
who have known waste and also favour:
time to come may find me eloquent

in other rooms, that reminisce
of this one so composed in silence. Love,
the necessary pain, has spurred a search.
Moving from place to place I always have
come some way closer to knowing
the final sequence of song that's going
to master the solitudes night can teach.

At Rest from the Grim Place

The sergeant laughs with strong teeth,
his jackboots nestle under the springbok horns.
Those bayonets are silent,
the spear of the nation gone to the ground.
Warriors prowl in the stars of their dungeons.
I've seen the nebulae of a man's eyes
squirm with pain, he sang his life
through cosmic volleys. They call it
genital therapy, the blond bosses.

Why is there no more news?
Bluetits scuffle in the eaves of England,
an easy summer shimmers on the water.
Fields of peace, I lie here
in the music of your gaze
so beautiful we seem no strangers.
Curling smoke, a white butt is
brother to my lips and fingers.
You watch the ash on grass blades gently crumble.
Your hands are small as roses,
they cancel memory.

Once going down to the sea through the mountains
my limbs felt freedom in the glide of air:
over the bridge at the window I found
speech an impossible cry.
Under the fatal shadows spun down the chasm
my heart squirmed in the throat of snaking water.
I have since forgotten what they call that place.

Mongane Wally Serote

The Growing

No!
This is not dying when the trees
Leave their twigs
To grow blindly long into windows like fingers into eyes.
And leave us unable
To wink or to blink or to actually close the eye,
The mind –
Twigs thrusting into windows and leaves falling on the sills,
Are like thoughts uncontrolled and stuffing the heart.
Yes,
This is teaching about the growing of things:
If you crowd me I'll retreat from you,
If you still crowd me I'll think a bit,
Not about crowding you but about your right to crowd me;
If you still crowd me, I will not, but I will be thinking
About crowding you.
If my thoughts and hands reach out
To prune the twigs and sweep the leaves,
There was a growth of thought here,
Then words, then action.
So if I say prune instead of cut,
I'm teaching about the growing of things.

Hell, Well, Heaven

I do not know where I have been,
But Brother,
I know I'm coming.
I do not know where I have been,
But Brother,
I know I heard the call.
Hell! where I was I cried silently
Yet I sat there until now.

I do not know where I have been,
But Brother,
I know I'm coming:
I come like a tide of water now,
But Oh! there's sand beneath me!
I do not know where I have been
To feel so weak, Heavens! so weary.
But Brother,
Was that Mankunku's* horn?
Hell! my soul aches like a body that has been beaten,
Yet I endured till now.
I do not know where I have been,
But Brother,
I know I'm coming.
I do not know where I have been,
But Brother I come like a storm over the veld,
And Oh! there are stone walls before me!
I do not know where I have been
To have fear so strong like the whirlwind (will it be that brief?)
But Brother,
I know I'm coming.
I do not know where I have been,
But Brother,
Was that Dumile's† figure?
Hell, my mind throbs like a heart beat, there's no peace;
And my body of wounds – when will they be scars? –
Yet I can still walk and work and still smile.
I do not know where I have been
But Brother,
I know I'm coming.
I do not know where I have been,
But Brother,
I have a voice like the lightning-thunder over the mountains.
But Oh! there are copper lightning conductors for me!
I do not know where I have been
To have despair so deep and deep and deep
But Brother,
I know I'm coming.

*Mankunku: a musician.   †Dumile: a sculptor.

I do not know where I have been
But Brother.
Was that Thoko's* voice?
Hell, well, Heavens!

*Thoko: a singer

Ofay-Watcher Looks Back

I want to look at what happened;
That done,
As silent as the roots of plants pierce the soil
I look at what happened,
Whether above the houses there is always either smoke or dust,
As there are always flies above a dead dog.
I want to look at what happened.
That done,
As silent as plants show colour: green,
I look at what happened,
When houses make me ask: do people live there?
As there is something wrong when I ask – is that man alive?
I want to look at what happened.
That done,
As silent as the life of a plant that makes you see it
I look at what happened
When knives creep in and out of people
As day and night into time.
I want to look at what happened,
That done,
As silent as plants bloom and the eye tells you:
                              something has happened
I look at what happened.
When jails are becoming necessary homes for people
Like death comes out of disease,

I want to look at what happened.

Uganda

Okot p'Bitek

From The *Song of Lawino* (1966)

Listen, my clansmen,
I cry over my husband
Whose head is lost.
Ocol has lost his head
In the forest of books.

When my husband
Was still wooing me
His eyes were still alive,
His ears were still unblocked,
Ocol had not yet become a fool
My friend was a man then!

He had not yet become a woman,
He was still a free man,
His heart was still his chief.

My husband was still a Black man
The son of the Bull
The son of Agik
The woman from Okol
Was still a man,
An Acoli. . . .

The papers on my husband's desk
Coil threateningly
Like the giant forest climbers,
Like the kituba tree
That squeezes other trees to death;
Some stand up,
Others lie on their backs,
They are inter-locked
Like the legs of youths
At the orak dance,
Like the legs of the planks

Of the goggo fence,
They are tightly interlocked
Like the legs of the giant forest climbers
In the impenetrable forest.

My husband's house
Is a mighty forest of books,
Dark it is and very damp,
The steam rising from the ground
Hot thick and poisonous
Mingles with the corrosive dew
And the rain drops
That have collected in the leaves. . . .

Oh, my clansmen,
Let us all cry together!
Come,
Let us mourn the death of my husband,
The death of a Prince
The Ash that was produced
By a great Fire!
O, this homestead is utterly dead,
Close the gates
With lacari thorns,
For the Prince
The heir to the Stool is lost!
And all the young men
Have perished in the wilderness!
And the fame of this homestead
That once blazed like wild fire
In a moonless night
Is now like the last breaths
Of a dying old man!

There is not one single true son left,
The entire village
Has fallen into the hands
Of war captives and slaves!
Perhaps one of our boys
Escaped with his life!
Perhaps he is hiding in the bush
Waiting for the sun to set!

But will he come?
Before the next mourning?
Will he arrive in time?

Bile burns my inside!
I feel like vomiting!
For all our young men
Were finished in the forest,
Their manhood was finished
In the class-rooms,
Their testicles
Were smashed
With large books!

From *Song of Prisoner* (1970)

Is today not my father's
Funeral anniversary?

My clansmen and clanswomen
Are gathering in our village,
They sit in circles
In the shades of granaries,
But who will make
The welcome speech?

Men drink kwete beer,
Women cook goat meat
And make millet bread,
But I am not there
To distribute the dishes
Among the elders!
The priests throw morsels
Of chicken meat,
They squirt goat blood
And pour libations
To the assembled ghosts
Of the dead,
But how can I address
The ghosts of my fathers
From here?

How can they put chymes
On my chest and back?
How can my grandmother
Spit blessing on me?

My age-mates have donned
White ostrich feathers,
They are singing a war song,
I want to join them
In the wilderness
And chase Death away
From our village,
Drive him a thousand miles
Beyond the mountains
In the west,
Let him sink down
With the setting sun
And never rise again.

I want to join
The funeral dancers,
I want to tread the earth
With a vengeance
And shake the bones
Of my father in his grave!

Zaïre

Antoine-Roger Bolamba

Portrait

I have my gri-gri
      gri-gri
      gri-gri
my calm bounding awake
clings to the wavy limbs of the Congo
never a stormy passage for my heart
bombarded with glowing oriflammes
I think of my silver necklace
become a hundred isles of silence
I admire the obstinate patience
of the okapi
bluebird battered in the open sky
what shipwreck
plunges it to the gulf of nothingness
nothingness empty of nightly entreaties

Ah! the broken resolutions
ah! the screaming follies
let my fate fall upon its guardians
they are three villains

I say three in counting 1 2 3
who dim the ancestral mirror
but you fugitive image
I will see you on the height of dizzy anger
wait while I put on my brow my mask of blood
and soon you will see
my tongue flutter like a banner.

A Fistful of News

The hills hunch their backs
and leap above the marshes
that wash about the calabash
of the Great Soul

Rumours of treason spread
like burning swords
the veins of the earth
swell with nourishing blood
the earth bears
towns villages hamlets
forests and woods
peopled with monsters horned and tentacled
their long manes are the mirror of the Sun

they are those who when night has come
direct the regiments of bats
and who sharpen their arms
upon the stone of horror.

the souls of the guilty
float in the currents of air
on the galleys of disaster
paying no heed to the quarrels of the earthbound
with fangs of fire
they tear from the lightning its diamond heart.

Surely the scorn is a gobbet of smoking flesh
surely the spirits recite the rosary of vengeance
but like the black ear of wickedness
they have never understood a single word
of the scorpion's obscure tongue:
stubbornness

nor the anger of the snake-wizard
nor the violence of the throwing-knife
can do anything against it.

Mukula Kadima-Nzuji

Incantations of the Sea: Moando Coast

Shocks of dizziness
my waves, my fears of the ocean
on the salty strand of my desire.

Shocks of carnal dreams
my heaps of loosened cliff
in the bitter absence
of sap mounting to the brim of the foam.

Loosened my pollens of drunkenness
and tied and retied my seaweeds
milky way of destinies.

And I hear
stooped over the virgin insomnia
of altitudes
the savage cries of the sea
and the rough backwash of my being.

Love in the Plural

neither this sobbing ocean
in the moon of your swelling voice
nor the milky vapour
on the window of my waking
nor this flood of men
in the margin of my shadow
which yearns for a safe shelter
nor the slipstreams on camelback
in the desert of my solitude
nor the spindrift nor the seaweeds
pillows for my storm-filled head
are able to decipher
where I inspect myself in vain
the reverse side of mirrors.

Notes on the Authors

Notes on the Authors

AIG-IMOUKHUEDE, FRANK: b.1935 at Ebunabon, near Ile-Ife, Nigeria. Attended Igbobi College and University College, Ibadan, where he contributed to J. P. Clark's poetry magazine *The Horn*. Has spent most of his career in information. One of the few poets since Adelaide Casely-Hayford to write poetry in Pidgin.

AIYEJINA, FUNSO: b.approx. 1950 in Western Nigeria. Studied at Ibadan University, Acadia University in Canada and University of the West Indies. Teaches in Department of Literature in English at Ife University. Has written many short stories, radio plays and poems. Some of his work has appeared in *Okike*, *Greenfield Review* and *Opon Ifa*.

ANDRADE, COSTA: b.1936 at Huambo, Angola. Studied architecture in Lisbon and Yugoslavia and was a leading figure in the Case dos Estundantes do Império. Served with M.P.L.A. guerrillas from 1968 to 1974. Has published poetry, short stories and criticism, including: *Terra de acácias rubras* (Lisbon, 1961); *Tempo Angolan em Italia* (Sao Paolo, 1963); *O Regresso e o Canto* (Lobito, 1975); *Poesia com Armas* (Lisbon, 1975); *O Caderno dos Heróis* (Luanda, 1977).

ANYIDOHO, KOFI: b.1947 at Wheta, Ghana. Trained as a teacher before entering University of Ghana to read English and Linguistics. Whilst in the U.S.A. for higher studies has published *Elegy for the Revolution* (1980). His poetry has also appeared in *Okike*, *Chi'ndaba* and *West Africa*.

ASALACHE, KHADAMBI: b.1934 at Kaimosi, Kenya. Studied art and architecture in Nairobi and Vienna, then worked in London for several years. Has published a novel, *A Calabash of Life* (Longmans, 1967).

AWOONOR, KOFI: b.1935 at Wheta, Ghana. Studied at Achimota, University of Ghana, London and New York. Edited the literary review *Okyeame* in the early sixties. After the fall of Kwame Nkrumah, spent some ten years in Britain and the U.S.A. before returning to Ghana in 1976 and joining University of Cape Coast. Has published *Rediscovery* (Ibadan, Mbari, 1964); *Night of My Blood* (Doubleday, 1971); *Ride Me, Memory* (Greenfield Review Press, 1973); *The House By the Sea* (Greenfield Review Press, 1978); a study of Ewe traditional poetry, *Guardians of the Sacred Word* (Nok Publications, 1974); a novel, *This Earth, My Brother* (Doubleday, 1971); and a study of African traditional culture, *The Breast of the Earth* (Doubleday, 1972).)

BA, OUMAR: b.1900 in Mauretania; has published many studies and translations of Peul poetry, including *Poèmes peuls modernes*. His French poetry was collected in *Paroles plaisantes au coeur et à l'oreille* (la Pensée Universelle, 1977).

BOGNINI, JOSEPH MIEZAN: b.1936 at Grand Bassam, Ivory Coast. Studied architecture in Paris. Published his poetry in *Ce dur appel de l'espoir* (Presence Africaine, 1960) and *Herbe féconde* (P. J. Oswald, 1973), as well as many individual poems in *Présence Africaine*.

BOLAMBA, ANTOINE-ROGER: b.1913 in Zaïre. Published many poems and articles in the journal *La Voix du congolais*, which he edited. Published *Esanzo* (Présence Africaine, 1956).

BREW, KWESI: b.1928 at Cape Coast, Ghana. Studied at University of Ghana and worked for many years as a diplomat. Published his poetry in *Shadows of Laughter* (Longmans, 1968) and in *Okyeame*.

BRUTUS, DENNIS: b.1924 in Zimbabwe. Taught for many years in South Africa and campaigned against racism in sport, being himself a keen sportsman. Shot in Johannesburg by South African police and jailed for eighteen months. After leaving Robben Island he was 'banned' and went to London in 1966. Now a Professor at North-Western University, Chicago. Many of his volumes of poetry were collected in *A Simple Lust* (Heinemann, 1973).

CHENEY-COKER, SYL.: b.1945 in Freetown, Sierra Leone. Studied there and in the U.S.A. Has been a drummer, journalist and radio producer, before turning to teaching. Moved to University of Maiduguri, Nigeria in 1978. Has published two volumes of poetry, *Concert for an Exile* (Heinemann, 1973) and *The Graveyard also has Teeth* (Heinemann, 1980). A third volume, *The Blood in the Desert's Eyes* is in preparation.

CLARK, J. P.: b.1935 in the Delta area of Nigeria. Studied at Government College, Ughelli, and University College, Ibadan, where he founded the poetry magazine *The Horn* in the 1950s. Taught for many years at Lagos University. Well known as a poet, dramatist, critic and translator. Many of his earlier poems were collected in *A Decade of Tongues* (Longmans, 1981). His translation of the Ijaw classic, *The Ozidi Saga*, is a major contribution to the study of African oral literature.

CRAVEIRIÑHA, JOSÉ: b.1922 at Lourenzo Marques, Mozambique. Worked for many years as a journalist before joining F.R.E.L.I.M.O. His poetry has appeared in many journals and anthologies, including Andrade's.

DE SOUSA, NOÉMIA: b.1927 at Lourenzo Marques, Mozambique. Very active in the liberation struggle in its early years, she later left Mozambique and lived quietly in exile. Her poetry has been widely published in literary journals and anthologies, including Andrade's.

DIOP, BIRAGO: b.1906 at Dakar, Senegal. Studied at Lycée Faidherbe in St Louis and later qualified as a veterinary surgeon. Spent much of his life in Upper Volta as a government veterinary officer. His output is small, but carefully and exquisitely composed. Has several poems in Senghor's anthology. Has published *Leurres et lueurs*, (Présence Africaine, 1960), *Les Contes d'Amadou Koumba* (Fasquelle, 1947), *Les Nouveaux Contes d'Amadou Koumba* (Présence Africaine, 1958). The last two volumes are French versions of the folk-tales of a famous storyteller.

DIOP, DAVID: b.1927 at Bordeaux of a Senegalese father and a Cameroonian mother. Killed in an air-crash off Dakar in 1960. Throughout his short life Diop was in poor health and was often in hospital. Moved frequently from his childhood onwards between France and West Africa. Was a regular contributor to *Présence Africaine* and had several early poems in Senghor's anthology. Published *Coups de pilon*, poems (Présence Africaine, 1956).

DIPOKO, MBELLA SONNE: b.1936 at Mungo, Cameroun. Educated in West Cameroun and Nigeria. Left for Paris in 1960 and has lived there ever since, devoting himself mainly to poetry and painting. Has published two novels, *A Few Nights and Days* (Longmans, 1966) and *Because of Women* (Heinemann 1974). Was a frequent contributor to *Transition* and *Présence Africaine*. Published his poetry in *Black and White in Love* (Heinemann, 1972).

DONGALA, EMMANUEL: b.1941 in Congo Republic. Has published poems in several journals and a novel, *Un fusil dans la main, un poeme dans la pôche* (Albin Michel, 1973).

ECHERUO, MICHAEL: b.1937 in Eastern Nigeria and educated at University College, Ibadan. Has held many academic posts in Nigeria and is currently Vice-Chancellor of the Imo State University. Published his first collection, *Mortality*, with Longmans in 1968.

HIGO, AIG: b.1942 in Mid-Western Nigeria. Studied at Ibadan University. After some years teaching, joined Heinemann and rose to become Managing Director of the Nigerian company. Contributed frequently to *Transition* and *Black Orpheus*.

JACINTO, ANTONIO: b.1924 in Luanda, Angola. Was a pioneer in the movement of cultural nationalism which preceded the armed struggle. Sentenced to fourteen years imprisonment for being an M.P.L.A. militant. Escaped from Portugal 1973 to join ranks of M.P.L.A. and served in government from 1975 onwards. Published *Poemas*, Lisbon, 1961.

JEMIE, ONWUCHEKWA: b.1940 at Item in Imo State, Nigeria. Studied at Columbia and Harvard universities in the U.S.A. Taught both at Columbia and Minnesota before returning to Nigeria. Currently working as a journalist in Lagos. His first book of poems, *Voyage*, was published by Papua Pocket Poets in 1971 and he has frequently appeared in *Okike*. Is co-author of *Towards the Decolonization of African Literature*, Enugu, 1980.

KADIMA-NZUJI, MUKULA: b.1947 at Lumumbashi, Zaïre. Member of a family prominent in literature and affairs. Has published *les Ressacs*, Kinshasa, 1969; *Préludes à la terre*, Kinshasa, 1971; and *Redire les mots anciens*, Paris, 1977.

KARIARA, JONATHAN: b.1938 in Kikuyuland, Kenya. Educated at Makerere University, where he began publishing many poems and short stories. Has worked for many years with publishers in Nairobi and contributes regularly to *Zuka*.

KAYO, PATRICE: b.1942 in the Bamileke country of N.W. Cameroun. Many of his poems have appeared in *Presence Africaine*. Has published *Hymnes et sagesses*, Paris, 1970; *Paroles intimes*, Paris, 1972; and *Chansons populaires Bamilekés*. Yaoundé, n.d.

KGOTSITSILE, KEORAPETSE: b.1938 in Johannesburg, South Africa. Has lived for many years in the U.S.A. and published most of his work there, apart from several poems in *Okike* and *Transition*. He was a pioneer of the more angry and abrupt style which later appeared in the work of Serote, Sepamla and others.

KOMEY, ELLIS AYITEY: b.1927 in Accra, Ghana, where he attended Accra Academy. Sometime editor of *Flamingo* magazine and a contributor to *Black Orpheus* and *West African Review*.

KUNENE, MAZISI: b.1932 in Durban, South Africa, where he took an M.A. Came to England in 1959 and worked for African National Congress whilst continuing his study of Zulu poetry. His own work is usually composed in Zulu and then translated into English by the poet himself. Since the middle seventies he has been a Professor of African Literature at the University of California, Los Angeles. His books include *Zulu Poems*, Deutsch, 1970, *Emperor Shaka the Zulu*, London, 1979 and *Anthem of the Decades*, London, 1981.

MALANGATANA, VALENTE: b.1936 at Marracuene, Mozambique and began drawing at an early age. His mother went mad when he was a child and his father was usually away at the mines in South Africa. After joining the studio of the architect Amancio Guedes he developed as a painter of great power and originality. His poems appeared in *Black Orpheus* during the sixties.

MAPANJE, JACK: b.1945? at Kadango, Southern Malawi. Studied at Malawi and London universities and became a Lecturer at Chancellor College, Zomba. A founder and editor of ODI, a journal of Malawi literature (founded 1971) and a contributor to *MAU: 39 Poems from Malawi* (Blantyre, 1971). First collection, *Of Chameleons and Gods*, published by Heinemann in 1981.

MAUNICK, EDOUARD: b.1931 at Port Louis, Mauritius, where he published his first volume, *Ces oiseaux de sang* before leaving for Paris, where he worked for several years with *Présence Africaine*. His major collection, *Les Manèges de la mer*, was published by Présence Africaine in 1964.

MNTHALI, FELIX: b.1933 in Northern Malawi. Studied at Malawi and Cambridge universities. Visited Ibadan University, Nigeria 1960–61, where he wrote *Echoes from Ibadan* (privately published). Since returning to Malawi, where he became Head of the Department of English, he has moved to Botswana.

MPONDO, SIMON: b.1935? in East Cameroun. Sometime lecturer at the College Libermann, Douala. Several of his poems have appeared in *Présence Africaine*.

MTSHALI, OSWALD: b.1940 in Natal, South Africa. Worked in various menial capacities. His first book of poems, *Sounds of a Cowhide Drum*, published in 1971 by Renoster Books, made a profound impression as one of the first manifestations of the new angry, energetic and biting voices of Black South Africa.

NDU, POL N: b.1940 in Eastern Nigeria. Studied at Nsukka and University of

298

New York. Several of his poems appeared in *Black Orpheus* and *Okike* and his first collection, *Songs for Seers*, was published by Nok in 1974. Tragically killed in a traffic accident in 1978, shortly after his return to Nigeria.

NETO, AUGUSTINHO: b.1922 in Icolo e Bengo region of Angola, his parents being school teachers and Methodists. After secondary school studies, worked in the colonial health services 1944–7, before going to Coimbra University, Portugal, to study medicine. First arrested 1951 for three months and again in 1952 for joining the Portuguese Movement for Democratic Youth Unity. Arrested again in 1955, he was held till 1957, when, in response to great public pressure, he was released to complete his medical studies. Returned to Angola in 1959 to practise medicine and to lead the underground M.P.L.A. Arrested again in 1960, he was held in Cape Verde Islands and Portugal, whence he escaped in 1962 to assume leadership of the armed struggle against colonial rule. At Angolan independence in 1975 he became President and held the post till his death in 1979. Publications include *Poemas*, Lisbon, 1961 and *Sagrada Esperanca*, Lisbon, 1974; trans. *Sacred Hope*, Dar-es-Salaam, 1974.

NORTJE, K. ARTHUR: b.1942 in Cape Province, South Africa. Attended government high school for Coloureds and taught until 1965, when he went to Jesus College, Oxford, to read English. After teaching in Canada, he returned to Oxford for a higher degree, but took his own life in 1970. His poetry first appeared in *Black Orpheus* in 1961 and he was awarded an Mbari Poetry Prize. His poems were edited and published posthumously by Heinemann as *Dead Roots*, 1973.

OFEIMUN, ODIA: b.1950 in Mid-Western Nigeria. Studied at Ibadan, where he published frequently in *Opon Ifa*, the Ibadan Poetry Chapbooks edited by Femi Osofisan. Took up political service in 1979. His first collection, *The Poet Lied*, was published by Longmans in 1980.

OGUNDIPE-LESLIE, MOLARA: b.194? in Western Nigeria. Studied at Ibadan University where she now teaches literature.

OKAI, ATUKWEI: b.1941 at Accra, Ghana. Took an M.A. at Gorky Literary Institute, Moscow and an M.Phil. in London before returning to Ghana to lecture in Russian at the University. He became President of the Ghana Association of Writers and gave many public readings of his poetry, of which he has published four volumes to date.

OKARA, GABRIEL: b.1921 beside the River Nun in the Niger Delta. After secondary schooling he trained as a binder and worked in the Government Printery at Enugu, where he began to write plays and poetry for radio. Was the first Nigerian poet to appear in *Black Orpheus* (1957). For several years before, during and after the civil war, he served in information and was the first editor of the *Nigerian Tide* newspaper. His collected poems, *The Fisherman's Invocation*, were published by Heinemann in 1978. His only novel, *The Voice*, appeared in 1964.

OKIGBO, CHRISTOPHER: b.1932 at Ojoto, in Eastern Nigeria. Educated at Government College, Umuahia, and University College, Ibadan, where he read Classics. Employed variously in the civil service, teaching, librarianship (at University of Nigeria, Nsukka) and publishing, he joined the Biafran army in 1967 and died in one of the first battles of the civil war near Nsukka, in September 1967. His poetic cycles *Heavensgate* (1960–62), *Limits* (1962) and *Distances* (1964) were first published in *Black Orpheus* or *Transition* and later by Mbari. The poems he wished to preserve were edited by Okigbo shortly before his death and published by Heinemann as *Labyrinths* in 1971, with his late sequence, *Paths of Thunder*, added. Okigbo's fastidiousness as a poet and the urgency of his lyrical voice have exercised a great – perhaps too great – an influence on some younger Nigerian poets, who find it difficult to escape from his shadow.

OLOGOUDOU, EMILE: b.1935 in Ouidah, Republic of Benin (formerly Dahomey). Studied law and sociology at University of Dakar 1957–60, then moved to University of Cologne 1960–66. Many of his poems have appeared in *Présence Africaine*.

OSUNDARE, NIYI: b.1947 in Ikere-Ekiti, Ondo State, Nigeria. Studied at Ibadan, Leeds and Toronto. Contributes frequently to *Opon Ifa* and *West Africa*. Lectures in English at Ibadan University, where he has also written several plays.

P'BITEK, OKOT: b.1931 in Gulu, Northern Uganda. Educated at Gulu High School and King's College, Budo, where he wrote and produced an opera. Whilst teaching near Gulu, he played football for Uganda and wrote a novel in Lwo, *Lak Tar Miyo Kinyero Wi Lobo* (If your Teeth are White, Laugh!) in 1953. Later studied law in Aberystwyth and social anthropology in Oxford, where he completed a B.Litt. thesis on the traditional songs of Acoli and Lango. Returning to Uganda he worked for some years in extra-mural studies, founding both the Gulu and Kisumu Arts Festivals. *Song of Lawino* was first composed in Lwo in rhyming couplets and was translated into English in 1966. The Lwo original was also published in 1971. It was followed by *Song of Ocol* (1970) and *Two Songs* (1971), all published by East African Publishing House. He also published a collection of Acoli traditional songs, *The Horn of My Love* (1974) and of Acoli folk-tales, *Hare and Hornbill* (1978). Okot's vigorous and direct poetry exercised an enormous influence throughout Africa. He spent the Amin years in exile and died in 1982, after returning to Uganda.

PETERS, LENRIE: b.1932 in Bathurst (now Banjul) in Gambia. Educated in Freetown and Cambridge, where he read medicine. Well-known as a singer and broadcaster. His first volume of poems was published by Mbari in 1964. In the same year, Heinemann published his novel *The Second Round*. His later volumes, both published by Heinemann, are *Satellites* (1967) and *Katchikali* (1971). Now practises as a surgeon in Banjul.

RABÉARIVELO, JEAN-JOSEPH: b.1901 in Antananarivo, Madagascar, of an impoverished noble family. Left school at thirteen and began writing poetry influenced by the French Symbolists. Founded a literary review and led the literary revival which swept Madagascar in the 1920s and 1930s. Several of his poems appeared in Senghor's anthology in 1948. Passionate and restless in temperament, he drifted from one job to another. He became a drug addict and killed himself in 1937, his despair exacerbated by the refusal of the French authorities to let him travel to France. He published *La Coupe des cendres* (1924), *Sylves* (1927), *Volumes* (1928) and *Presques-songes* (1934). An English translation of some of his works, *24 Songs*, was published by Mbari in 1963 and Heinemann issued *Translations from the Night* a few years later.

RANAIVO, FLAVIEN: b.1914 in Imerina, near Antananarivo, Madagascar, his father being Governor of Arivonimamo. Did not go to school until he was eight and learnt to read music before the alphabet. Since early childhood has spent much time wandering through the countryside, studying its music, his poetry being much influenced by popular song and ballad forms, especially that called *hain-teny*. His example was important in rooting the new Francophone poetry of Madagascar more deeply in its indigenous poetry and song. Several of his poems appeared in Senghor's anthology. Has published *L'Ombre et le vent* (1947) and *Mes chansons de toujours* (1955).

REBELO, JORGE: b.1940 in Lourenzo Marques, Mozambique. Lawyer and journalist, he joined F.R.E.L.I.M.O. and became its Director of Information during the war of liberation. His poems appeared in *Breve Antologia de Literatura Mozambicana*, published by F.R.E.L.I.M.O. in 1967.

ROCHA, JOFRE: b.1941 in Cachimane near Luanda, Angola. Arriving in Lisbon to study in 1961, he was arrested at the airport and held there and in Luanda until 1963. Joined M.P.L.A. and was soon re-arrested, being held until 1968. At independence in 1975, became Director-General of External Relations and then Deputy Minister in the same department. In 1978 he became Minister of External Trade. Has published *Tempo do Cicio*, Lobito, 1973; *Estórias de Musseque*, Luanda, 1977 and *Assim se fez Madrugada*, Luanda, 1977.

RUBADIRI, JAMES DAVID: b.1930 in Central Nyasaland (now Malawi). Studied at Makerere College in Uganda, was arrested in the Nyasaland crisis of 1959 but went to Cambridge after his release and read English. Was Ambassador in Washington and New York until 1965, when he returned to Makerere and moved later to Nairobi as a university lecturer. His first novel, *No Bride Price*, was published in Nairobi in 1967. Many of his poems have appeared in *Transition*.

SANTO, ALDO DO ESPIRITO: b.1926 in San Tomé, where he worked for many years as a teacher. His poems appeared in Andrade's anthology and in several Portuguese reviews.

SENGHOR, LÉOPOLD SÉDAR: b.1906 in Joal, Senegal, his father being a groundnut merchant and a Roman Catholic in a predominantly Muslim land. Senghor passed brilliantly through the *lycée* in Dakar and went to the Lycée Louis le Grand in Paris in 1928. Later he completed his *agrégation* at the Sorbonne, the first West African to do so. In Paris he met Césaire and Damas with whom he formulated the movement of black cultural assertion known as *négritude*. Before independence, he was variously a Deputy for Senegal in the

French National Assembly, a Minister in the French Government and a member of the Council of Europe. In 1960 he became the first President of Senegal, holding that post until his retirement in 1981. Throughout his long career in politics, Senghor retained his immense prestige as a pioneer in the re-assertion of African cultural values and as the doyen of African poets in French. His style emerged fully formed in his first book, filled with the sombre melody of his long lines and his favourite imagery of the night and the moon, of tender and protective spiritual presences. All his major volumes of poetry have been published by Éditions du Seuil in Paris and include *Chants d'ombres* (1945), *Hosties noires* (1958), *Éthiopiques* (1956) and *Nocturnes* (1961). His collected poems were issued by the same publishers in 1964.

SEPAMLA, SIPHO: b.1932 in Johannesburg, where he has lived all his life. Is now editor of the magazine *New Classic*, which has published much of the new South African black poetry. His own volumes include *Hurry up to it!* 1975, *The Blues is You in Me*, 1976 and *The Soweto I Love*, 1977.

SEROTE, MONGANE WALLY: b.1944 in Sophiatown, Johannesburg and has lived all his life in the city. Imprisoned for nine months under the Terrorism Act in 1969–70. Many of his early poems appeared in *The Classic* and *Purple Renoster*. Renoster Books issued his first book of poems, *Yakhal 'inkomo*, in 1972.

SILVEIRA, ONÉSIMA: b.1936 in Cape Verde Islands. Lived for some years in San Tomé and Angola. Joined the liberation movement of Cape Verde and Guinea, the P.A.I.G.C., and became its representative in Sweden. His first collection was entitled *Hora Grande*.

SOYINKA, WOLE: b.1934 in Abeokuta, Western Nigeria. Studied at Government College, Ibadan, University College, Ibadan and at Leeds University. Taught for a while in London and worked at Royal Court Theatre, which presented an evening of his theatrical sketches and songs. His first plays, *The Swamp Dwellers* and *The Lion and the Jewel*, were produced in London in 1959. In 1960 he returned to Nigeria and threw himself into a period of intense activity as writer, actor and producer. Although chiefly known as Africa's leading dramatist, Soyinka has achieved considerable prominence as a novelist, essayist, poet and teacher (he has headed Theatre Arts Departments at both Ibadan and Ife universities) His early poems appeared in *Black Orpheus* in 1959. In 1967 he published *Idanre and Other Poems*. A small collection, *Poems from Prison*, was published by Rex Collings during his imprisonment in Northern Nigeria 1967–9, and a major collection of poems written then appeared as. *A Shuttle in the Crypt* in 1972. A long narrative poem, *Ogun Abibiman*, was published by Opon Ifa in 1976 and by Rex Collings in 1977. Soyinka also edited *Transition/Ch'indaba* in Accra 1973–76.

TATI-LOUTARD, JEAN-BAPTISTE: b.1939 in Ngoyo, Congo Republic. Educated at Pointe Noire, Brazzaville and Bordeaux, where he studied Modern Literature and Italian, writing a thesis on Benedetto Croce. Whilst in France, published his first two volumes of poetry, *Poèmes de la mer* (Yaoundé, 1968) and *Les Racines congolaises* (P. J. Oswald, 1968). His later volumes include

L'Envers du soleil (P. J. Oswald, 1970) and *Les Normes du temps* (Lumumbashi, 1974). After teaching at the University of Brazzaville, he joined the government as Minister of Culture.

TIDJANI-CISSÉ, AHMED: b.1947 in Conakry, Guinea. Left Guinea in 1963 and studied law and political science in Paris, where he is a Professor of African Dance and Director of an African ballet troupe. Has recently published a play, *Maudit soit Cham*, with Éditions Nubia, which also published his poems, *Pollens et fleurs*, in 1980. The latter won the prize 'Poésie Plurielle' in 1981.

U TAM'SI, TCHICAYA: b.1931 in Mpili, Congo Republic. In 1946 accompanied his father, then Deputy for Congo, to France and studied in Orleans and Paris. In addition to his many volumes of poetry, has written many radio features, plays and stories. His first novel, *Les Concrelats*, was published by Albin Michel in 1980 and a collection of stories, *La Main sèche*, by Juillard in the same year. Apart from a short spell in Kinshasa as editor of a newspaper during the Lumumba era, Tchicaya has lived in France since his childhood, but his work with U.N.E.S.C.O. enables him to visit the African continent frequently. His first volume *Le Mauvais Sang* was published in 1955 and was reissued with *Feu de brousse* and *À triche-coeur* by P. J. Oswald in 1970. Oswald also reissued *L'Arc musical* and *Épitomé* in the same year. More recently Tchicaya has published *La Veste d'interieur* with Éditions Nubia 1978, and an expanded edition of *Le Ventre* with Présence Africaine, also in 1978. An English translation of *Feu de brousse* was published by Mbari in 1964, whilst Gerald Moore's *Selected Poems of Tchicaya U Tam'si*, published by Heinemann in 1970, contains the whole of *À triche-coeur* and *Épitomé*, together with selections from *Le Ventre* and *L'Arc musical*. Undoubtedly the major Francophone poet now writing.

WENDEL, NGUDIA: b.1940 in Icolo e Bengo region, near Luanda, Angola. Has spent his whole adult life with M.P.L.A., first as a guerrilla leader and later, after training in the Soviet Union, as a doctor. In 1973–4 was Director of Medical Services on the Northern Front and in Cabinda. His collection *Nos Volteramos, Luanda!* (We shall Return, Luanda!) was published in Lusaka in 1970 and in a bilingual Portuguese–Italian edition at Forli in 1974.

WONODI, OKOGBULE: b.1936 in Port Harcourt, Eastern Nigeria. After training as a teacher, studied and taught at Nsukka. Later attended the Writers' Workshop at Iowa University. Under the last military regime in Nigeria 1975–9, he was for some years Chairman of Port Harcourt Town Council. His first volume, *Ucheke*, was published by Mbari in 1964 and he contributed frequently to *Black Orpheus*.

YAMBO, OUOLOGUEM: b.1940 in the Dogon country of Mali Republic, only son of a school inspector. Went to Paris in 1962 to study philosophy, literature and sociology. His first novel, *Le Devoir de violence*, won the Prix Renaudot in 1968. This was followed by the vigorous satirical pamplet, *Lettre ouverte a la France-nègre*, addressed to General de Gaulle. His poetry has not been collected, but several poems appeared in *Nouvelle somme*.

Sources of the Poems

AIG-IMOUKHUEDE: from MS.

AIYEJINA: from MS.

ANDRADE: from *Poems from Angola, q.v.*

ANYIDOHO: from *West Africa*, 14 June 1982, and *Elegy for the Revolution* (Greenfield Review Press, 1980).

ASALECHE: from MS.

AWOONOR: 'Songs of Sorrow', 'Song of War', and 'The Sea Eats the Land at Home' from *Okyeame*, 1 (Accra, 1961); 'Lover's Song', 'The Weaver Bird' and 'Easter Dawn' from *Rediscovery* (Ibadan, Mbari Publications, 1964); 'At the Gates' from *Night of My Blood* (Doubleday, 1971); 'Afro-American Beats' from *Ride Me, Memory* (Greenfield Review Press, 1973); 'The First Circle' from *The House by the Sea* (Greenfield Review Press, 1978).

BA: from *Paroles plaisantes au coeur et à l'oreille* (la Pensée Universelle, 1977).

BOGNINI: 'My Days Overgrown' (trans. Ulli Beier) from *Black Orpheus*, 18, 1965; 'Earth and Sky' from *Ce dur appel de l'espoir* (Présence Africaine, 1960). Other poems (trans. Gerald Moore) from *Herbe féconde* (P. J. Oswald, 1973).

BOLAMBA: from *Esanzo* (Présence Africaine, 1956): trans. Gerald Moore

BREW: from *Okyeame*, 1 (Accra, 1961)

BRUTUS: first three poems from *Sirens, Knuckles, Boots* (Ibadan, Mbari Publications, 1963); Poems About Prison 1 from *A Simple Lust* (Heinemann, 1973).

CHENEY-COKER: first six poems from *The Graveyard also Has Teeth* (Heinemann, 1980); 'The Philosopher' from MS.

CLARK: first five poems from *Poems* (Ibadan, Mbari Publications, 1962); 'A Child Asleep' from *Black Orpheus*, 13, 1963; 'The Leader' from *A Reed in the Tide* (Longmans, 1965); 'Season of Omens' from *Casualties* (Longmans, 1970).

CRAVEIRIÑHA: from Andrade's anthology, *q.v.*

DE SOUSA: 'Appeal' from Andrade's anthology, *q.v.*; 'If You want to Know Me' (trans. Art Brakel) from *Ba Shiru* (Madison, Wisconsin, Spring 1970).

DIOP (BIRAGO): all poems from *Leurres et lueurs* (Présence Africaine, 1960): trans. Gerald Moore and Ulli Beier.

DIOP (DAVID): all poems from *Coups de pilon* (Présence Africaine, 1956): trans. Gerald Moore and Ulli Beier.

DIPOKO: 'Pain' and revised version of 'Exile' from MS. 'Our Life' from *Transition*, Vol. 4, No. 10, 1963; other poems from *Black and White in Love* (Heinemann, 1972)

DONGALA: from *Nouvelle Somme, q.v.*: trans. Gerald Moore.

ECHERUO: 'Melting Pot' from *Black Orpheus*, 12 (Ibadan, 1963); 'Man and God Distinguished' from *Mortality* (Longmans, 1968).

HIGO: 'Ritual Murder' from *Transition*, Vol. 3, No. 8, 1963; 'Hidesong' from *Transition*, Vol. 3, No. 9, 1963.

JACINTO: 'Monongamba' from Andrade's anthology, *q.v.*; other poems from *Poems from Angola*, *q.v.*

JEMIE: from *Voyage* (Ife, Papua Pocket Poets, 1971).

KADIMA-NZUJI: from *Présence Africaine*, 97, 1976: trans. Gerald Moore.

KARIÁRA: from *Zuka*, 1, Nairobi.

KAYO: 'Song of the Initiate' from *Nouvelle Somme*, *q.v.* 'War' from *Paroles intimes* (P. J. Oswald, 1972) both trans. Gerald Moore.

KGOTSITSILE: 'The Air I Hear' from MS., 'Song for Ilva Mackay and Mongane' from *Transition/Ch'indaba*, 2, 1976; 'The Present is a Dangerous Place to Live' from *Okike*, 3 (Amherst, Massachusetts, 1972).

KOMEY: 'The Change' from *Black Orpheus*, 9, 1961; 'Oblivion' from *Messages*, ed. Awoonor and Adali-Morty (Heinemann, 1971).

KUNENE: 'The Echoes' and 'Elegy' from MS., 'Thought on June 26' from *Poems of Black Africa*, *q.v.*

MALANGATANA: from *Black Orpheus* trans. Dorothy Guedes.

MAPANJE: from *Of Chameleons and Gods* (Heinemann, 1981).

MAUNICK: from *Les Manèges de la mer* (Présence Africaine, 1964): trans. Gerald Moore.

MNTHALI: from *Echoes from Ibadan* (Ibadan, privately printed, 1961).

MPONDO: from *Présence Africaine*, 93, 1975.

MTSHALI: from *Sounds of a Cowhide Drum* (Johannesburg, Renoster Books, 1971).

NDU: 'udude' from *Black Orpheus*, 18, 1965; 'Evacuation' from *Songs for Seens* (Nok Publications, 1974).

NETO: 'Farewell at the Moment of Parting' (trans. Gerald Moore) from Andrade's anthology, *q.v.*; 'African Poem' and 'Kinaxixi' (trans. W. S. Merwin) from *Black Orpheus*, 15, 1964; 'The Grieved Lands of Africa' from *Poems from Angola*, *q.v.*

NOKAN: from *Nouvelle Somme*, *q.v.* trans. Gerald Moore.

NORTJE: from MS.

OFEIMUN: from *The Poet Lied* (Longmans, 1980).

OGUNDIPE-LESLIE: from *Okike*, 21, 1982

OKAI: from *Poems of Black Africa*, *q.v.*

OKARA: first two poems from *Reflections*, *q.v.*; 'Adhiambo' and 'One Night at Victoria Beach' from MS. 'Spirit of the Wind' from *Black Orpheus*, 1, 1957.

OKIGBO: first seven poems from *Heavensgate* (Ibadan, Mbari Publications, 1961); next four poems from *Limits* (Ibadan, Mbari Publications, 1962; two movements of *Distances* from *Transition*, Vol. 4, No. 16, 1964; one movement of *Lament of the Drums* from *Labyrinths* (Heinemann, 1961); *Come Thunder* from *Black Orpheus*, Vol. II, No. 1, 1967.

OLOGOUDOU: from *Nouvelle somme, q.v.*; trans. Gerald Moore.

OSUNDARE: from *I Sing of Change* (Ibadan, privately printed, 1981).

PETERS: 'Homecoming', from *Black Orpheus*, 11, 1962; 'One Long Jump' and 'Parachute Men' from *Poems* (Ibadan, Mbari Publications, 1964); 'Isatou Died' from *Katchikali* (Heinemann, 1971).

P'BITEK: from *Song of Lawino* (Nairobi, East African Publishing House, 1966) and from *Song of Prisoner* in *Two Songs* (Nairobi, East African Publishing House, 1971).

RABÉARIVELO: all poems from Senghor's anthology; English translations by Ulli Beier and Gerald Moore from *24 Poems* (Ibadan, Mbari Publications, 1963).

RANAIVO: poems from Senghor's anthology, *q.v.*, trans. Gerald Moore.

REBELO: 'Poem' from *When Bullets Begin to Flower, q.v.*; 'Poem for a Militant' (trans. Art Brakel) from *Ba Shiru* (Madison, Wisconsin, Spring 1970).

ROCHA: from *Poems from Angola, q.v.*

RUBADIRI: from MS.

SANTO: from Andrade's anthology, *q.v.*; trans. Gerald Moore.

SENGHOR: all poems from *Poèmes* (Éditions du Seuil, 1964), trans. Gerald Moore and Ulli Beier.

SEPAMLA: all poems from *The Soweto I Love* (Rex Collings, 1977).

SEROTE: all poems from *Poets to the People*, ed. Barry Feinberg (Allen & Unwin, 1974).

SILVEIRA: from *When Bullets Begin to Flower, q.v.*

SOYINKA: 'Death in the Dawn' and 'Abiku' from *Black Orpheus*, 10, 1962; 'Massacre, October '66' and 'Civilian and Soldier' from *Idanre* (Eyre Methuen, 1967); 'Prisoner' from *Reflections, q.v.*; 'Season' from *Encounter*; 'Night' from MS., 'Ujamaa' and 'Amber Wall' from *A Shuttle in the Crypt* (Eyre Methuen, 1972).

TATI-LOUTARD: 'News of My Mother' from MS., 'The Voices', 'Submarine Tombs' and 'Pilgrimage to Loango Strand', from *Poèmes de la mer* (Yaoundé, Éditions Cléa, 1968); other poems from *Les Racines congolaises* (P. J. Oswald, 1968). All poems trans. Gerald Moore.

TIDJANI-CISSÉ: from *Pollens et fleurs* (Éditions Nubia, 1980), trans. Gerald Moore.

U TAM'SI: 'Brush-fire', 'Dance to the Amulets' and 'A Mat to Weave' from *Brushfire* (Ibadan, Mbari Publications, 1964), trans. Ulli Beier; all other poems from *Selected Poems* (Heinemann, 1970), trans. Gerald Moore.

WENDEL: from *Poems from Angola, q.v.*

WONODI: 'Planting' from *Ucheke* (Ibadan, Mbari Publications, 1964); 'Salute to Icheke' from *Black Orpheus*, 19, 1966.

YAMBO: from *Nouvelle Somme, q.v.*, trans. Gerald Moore.

N.B. The following works are frequently referred to above and marked *q.v.* for brevity of referencing:

(i) Andrade, Mario de, *Antologia de la poesia negra de espressão portuguesa* (Lisbon, 1953).

(ii) *Black Orpheus*: Journal of African and Afro-American Literature, founded and edited by Ulli Beier, published approximately twice yearly in Ibadan 1957–67. Second series edited by J. P. Clark and Abiola Irele, published occasionally in Lagos from 1968 onwards.

(iii) *Nouvelle somme de poésie du monde noir*, ed. Paolin Joachim (Présence Africaine, No. 57, 1966).

(iv) *Poems from Angola*, ed. and trans. Michael Wolfers (Heinemann, 1979), All trans. by the editor.

(v) *Poems of Black Africa*, ed. Wole Soyinka (Heinemann, 1975).

(vi) *Présence Africaine*, founded by Alioune Diop, published thrice yearly in Paris since 1947. Not to be confused with the publishing house of the same name.

(vii) *Reflections*, ed. Frances Ademola (Lagos, African Universities Press, 1962).

(viii) Senghor, L.S. *Nouvelle anthologie de la poésie nègre et malgache* (Presses Universitaires de la France, 1948).

(ix) *Transition*, founded and edited by Rajat Neogy, published thrice yearly in Kampala 1961–68 and in Accra 1971–76. Wole Soyinka became editor in 1973 and the last two issues were retitled *Ch'indaba*. Ceased publication 1976.

(x) *When Bullets Begin to Flower*, ed. and trans. Margaret Dickinson (Nairobi, East African Publishing House, 1972).

(xi) *Zuka*, literary journal published occasionally in Nairobi.

(xii) *Okike*, founded and edited by Chinua Achebe. Started in 1971, it still appears thrice yearly from Nsukka, Nigeria.

Index of First Lines

A leopard lives in a Muu tree   121
A poet alone in my country   249
A scroll of blue, an exquisite thought   241
A thousand ghosts haunt our souls in birth waters   104
Africa my Africa   245
All the wives of my father   55
All was quiet in this park   51
Amadu I live alone inside four walls of books   253
An ailing bird over the desert made its agony   51
An echo of childhood stalks before me   198
An image insists   182
And at the door of the eye   269
And the flower weeps unbruised   178
At home the sea is in the town   92
Autumnal skies   45

Banks of reed   181
Be not amazed beloved, if sometimes my song grows dark   238
Beaten up   151
Before bulging eyes   140
Before you, mother Idoto   176
Black as my night, anonymous here   96
Black, green and gold at sunset: pageantry   259
Black mask, red mask, you black and white masks   233
Black people are born singers   265
Blood falling in drops to the earth   225
Breath of the sun, crowned   194
Bright   177

Call her, call her for me, that girl   93
Clawed green-eyed   77
Cold   260
Come, brother and tell me your life   166
Come over here   63
Coming and going these several seasons   199

Dead or living   159
Death lay in ambush   184
Didn't you say we should trace   141
Distance   209
Do not tell me, my brother, to reach   270
Don't love me, my dear   134
Don't you know   151
Dzogbese Lisa has treated me thus   89

Earth and sky are infinities   114
Everyone thinks me a cannibal   147
Eyes of heavenly essence, O breasts of the purity of breasts   252
Eyes open on the beach   176

Far across the waves, the wing of a gull   70
Festive draperies override the claims of   218
For he was a shrub among the poplars   180
From flesh into phantom   183
From the west   137
Further off is the measured force the word of the sea   155

Grave number twenty-four   208
Grey, to the low grass cropping   191

He came to deliver the secret of the sun   64
He who plucked light   200
Hear now a sound of floods   268
His baby cry   273

I am now very high upon the tree of the seasons   70
I am standing above you and tide   179
I am tempted to think of you   52
I came to the east   41
I climbed towards you on a ray of moonlight   74
I do not know where I have been   277
I do not know which god sent me   94
I done try go church, I done go for court   203
I dream in the intimate semi-darkness of an afternoon   234
I drink to your glory my god   68
I have followed to this strand the scent of their blood   71
I have my gri-gri   289
I hear many voices   173

I love to encounter you in strange cities   159
I love to pass my fingers   195
I myself will be the stage for my salvation!   68
I sing   216
I struck tomorrow square in the face   217
I shall sleep in white calico   91
I thought of eden   266
I want to look at what happened   279
I want to remember the fallen palm   86
I wanted to write you a letter   35
I was counting time in the heartbeat of the storm   103
I was glad to sit down   29
I was naked for the first kiss of my mother   66
I will pronounce your name, Naëtt, I will declaim you, Naëtt!   238
I struck tomorrow square in the face   213
If a squirrel crosses my way   122
If we tell, gently, gently   240
If you want to know who I am   162
In one of the three pots   241
In silence   52
In the cabin   160
In the cool waters of the river   165
In those days   246
In vain your bangles cast   193
In your presence I rediscovered my name   244
Into your arms I came   164
Isatou died   82
Is today not my father's   285
It is a hive   271
It is dark, now, and grave   206
It is Sunday.   229

Let your wandering fingers   215
Let's talk to the swallows visiting us in summer   266
Lights on the shore   204
Like others I get drunk in my blood   254
Lion-hearted cedar forest, gonads for our thunder,   183
Listen comrades of the struggling centuries   243
Listen, my clansmen   283
Luanda, you are like a white seagull   38

Man sees the stars   207
May ours not be like the story   221
May the hide of the earth split beneath my feet   72
Mother   167
My apparition rose from the fall of lead   190
My brother you flash your teeth in response to every hypocrisy   244
My days overgrown with coffee blossoms   113
My dear son I am well thanks be to God   107
My head is immense   116
My mother   27

Neither this sobbing ocean   291
New York! At first I was confused by your beauty, by these great
   golden long-legged girls   235
Nine hundred and ninety-nine smiles   99
Night here, the owners asleep upstairs   274
No animals will live   213
No!   277
Now that the triumphant march has entered the last street
   corners   186

O Mzingeli son of the illustrious clans   263
Oaf   133
Old chronicler   210
On that big estate there is no rain   31
Once I was a lizard   125
One mustn't confuse the day and the night   152
One long jump   79
Open your palms   126
Over the vast summer hills   262

Parachute men say   81
Pavements lined   119

Royal blue azure blue   108
Rust is ripeness, rust   192

Shards of sunlight touch me here   189
She   130
Shocks of dizziness   291

Sleep well, my love, sleep well   259
So all waited for manna   124
So would I to the hills again   179
Solitude supporting solitude on two pergolas   250
Suddenly an old man on the threshold of the age   115
Suddenly becoming talkative   180
Sweating between his fingers, the agricultural man   251
Sweat is leaven for the earth   194

Tell me, before the ferryman's return   197
That man died in Jerusalem   93
That multitude of moulded hands   132
That we may have life   138
The air, I hear   267
The black glassmaker   131
The country of the dead   123
The fire the river that's to say   63
The flat end of sorrow here   97
The great dark work   211
The grieved lands of Africa   29
The hide of the black cow is stretched   130
The hills hunch their backs   290
The mystic drum beat in my inside   172
The past   88
The people of the islands want a different poem   59
The present reigned supreme   77
The price seemed reasonable, location   187
The prostitutes at Smiller's Bar beside the dusty road   143
The season of the rains   49
The sergeant laughs with strong teeth   275
The snowflakes sail gently   171
The spring has swept the ice from all my frozen rivers   232
The storks are coming now   174
The Sun hung by a thread   239
The weaver bird built in our house   93
The white carcases   46
The wind comes rushing from the sea   175
There are on the earth 50,000 dead whom no one mourned   37
There on the horizon   28
They are still so anthropologically tall here   143
They choose paths   217

They have felled him to the ground   201
They rode upon   272
Thirty centimes is all the money I have left   54
This is not yet my poem   32
This morning at the Luxembourg, this autumn at the Luxembourg,
   as I lived and relived my youth   231
This sun on this rubble after rain   260
Those questions, sister   139
Thundering drums and cannons   178
Thunderous vapours!   56
Today even those fireflies have become   142
Traveller, you must set out   188

Was I wrong when I thought   264
We are men of the new world a tree prompts us to harmony   115
We are this union   69
We charge through the skies of disillusion   214
We have come home   78
We have come to your shrine to worship   87
We who have listened to silences abort   220
What dark tempestuous night has been hiding your face?   238
What do I want with a thousand stars in broad daylight   66
What invisible rat   129
What tiem of night it is   196
When did I cease to be   205
When calabashes held petrol and men   201
When I return from the land of exile and silence   40
Who has strangled the tired voice   161
Who lived here when the stones were green   256
With a dozen blows the clock betrays the pulse of time   72
With my seven-fold inquisitorial eye   71
Without kings and warriors occasional verse fails   142
Woman, rest on my brow your balsam hands, your hands gentler than
   fur   230

You held the black face of the warrior between your hands   237
You must be from my country   67
You tell me you have right on your side?   151
Your hand is heavy, Night, upon my brow   196
Your infancy now a wall of memory   85
Your voice awakens   219

Acknowledgements

For permission to republish the poems in this anthology acknowledgement is made to the poets themselves and to the following copyright holders:

For Costa Andrade to Heinemann Educational Books; for Kofi Anyidoho to *West Africa* and Greenfield Review Press; for Kofi Awoonor to Mbari Publications, *Okyeame*, Doubleday and Co., and Greenfield Review Press; for Oumar Ba to la Pensée Universelle; for Joseph Miezan Bognini to Présence Africaine and P. J. Oswald; for Antoine-Roger Bolamba to Présence Africaine; for Kwesi Brew to *Okyeame*; for Dennis Brutus to Mbari Publications and Heinemann Educational Books; for Syl Cheney-Coker to Heinemann Educational Books; for J. P. Clark to Mbari Publications, *Black Orpheus* and Longmans; for Jose Craveirinha to P. J. Oswald; for Noémia de Sousa to P. J. Oswald and *Ba Shiru*; for Birago Diop to Présence Africaine; for David Diop to Présence Africaine; for Mbella Sonne Dipoko to *Transition* and Heinemann Educational Books; for Emmanuel Dongala to Présence Africaine; for Michael Echeruo to *Black Orpheus* and Longmans; for Aig Higo to *Transition*; for Antonio Jacinto to P. J. Oswald and Heinemann Educational Books; for Onwuchekwa Jemie to Papua Pocket Poets; for Mukula Kadima-Nzuji to Présence Africaine; for Patrice Kayo to Présence Africaine and P. J. Oswald; for Jonathan Kariara to *Zuka*; for Keorapetse Kgositsile to *Transition/Chi'ndaba* and *Okike*; for Ellis Ayitey Komey to *Black Orpheus* and Heinemann Educational Books; for Mazisi Kunene to Heinemann Educational Books; for Valente Malangatana to *Black Orpheus*; for Jack Mapanje to Heinemann Educational Books; for Edouard Maunick to Présence Africaine; for Simon Mpondo to Présence Africaine; for Oswald Mtshali to Renoster Books; for Pol Ndu to Black Orpheus and Nok Publications; for Augustinho Neto to P. J. Oswald, *Black Orpheus* and Heinemann Educational Books; for Charles Nokan to Présence Africaine; for Atukwai Okai to Heinemann Educational Books; for Gabriel Okara to African Universities Press and *Black Orpheus*; for Odia Ofeimun to Longmans; for Molara Ogundipe-Leglie to *Okike*; for Christopher Okigbo to Mbari Publications, *Transition* and Heinemann Educational Books; for Emile Ologoudou to Présence Africaine; for Lenrie Peters to *Black Orpheus*, Mbari Publications and Heinemann Educational Books; for Okot p'Bitek to East African Publishing House; for Jean-Joseph Rabéarivelo and Flavien Ranaivo to Presses Universitaires de la France; for Jorge Rebelo to East African Publishing House and *Ba Shiru*; for Jofre Rocha to Heinemann Educational Books; for Aldo do Espirito Santo to P. J. Oswald; for Léopold Sédar Senghor to Editions du Seuil and *Black Orpheus*; for Sipho Sepamla to Rex Collings; for Mongane Wally Serote to Allen & Unwin; for Onésima Silveira to East African Publishing House; for Wole Soyinka to *Black Orpheus*, Eyre Methuen, African Universities Press and *Encounter*; for Jean-Baptiste Tati-Loutard to Éditions Cléa and P. J. Oswald; for Ahmed Tidjani-Cissé to Nubia; for Tchicaya U Tam'si to Caractères, P. J. Oswald, *Black Orpheus* and Heinemann Educational Books; for Ngudia Wendel to Heinemann Educational Books; for Okogbule Wonodi to *Black Orpheus* and *Transition*; for Ouologuem Yambo to Présence Africaine.

Discover more about our forthcoming books through Penguin's FREE newspaper...

Penguin Quarterly

It's packed with:

- exciting features
- author interviews
- previews & reviews
- books from your favourite films & TV series
- exclusive competitions & much, much more...

READ MORE IN PENGUIN

In every corner of the world, on every subject under the sun, Penguin represents quality and variety – the very best in publishing today.

For complete information about books available from Penguin – including Puffins, Penguin Classics and Arkana – and how to order them, write to us at the appropriate address below. Please note that for copyright reasons the selection of books varies from country to country.

In the United Kingdom: Please write to *Dept. JC, Penguin Books Ltd, FREEPOST, West Drayton, Middlesex UB7 OBR*

If you have any difficulty in obtaining a title, please send your order with the correct money, plus ten per cent for postage and packaging, to *PO Box No. 11, West Drayton, Middlesex UB7 OBR*

In the United States: Please write to *Penguin USA Inc., 375 Hudson Street, New York, NY 10014*

In Canada: Please write to *Penguin Books Canada Ltd, 10 Alcorn Avenue, Suite 300, Toronto, Ontario M4V 3B2*

In Australia: Please write to *Penguin Books Australia Ltd, 487 Maroondah Highway, Ringwood, Victoria 3134*

In New Zealand: Please write to *Penguin Books (NZ) Ltd,182–190 Wairau Road, Private Bag, Takapuna, Auckland 9*

In India: Please write to *Penguin Books India Pvt Ltd, 706 Eros Apartments, 56 Nehru Place, New Delhi 110 019*

In the Netherlands: Please write to *Penguin Books Netherlands B.V., Keizersgracht 231 NL–1016 DV Amsterdam*

In Germany: Please write to *Penguin Books Deutschland GmbH, Friedrichstrasse 10–12, W–6000 Frankfurt/Main 1*

In Spain: Please write to *Penguin Books S. A., C. San Bernardo 117–6º E–28015 Madrid*

In Italy: Please write to *Penguin Italia s.r.l., Via Felice Casati 20, I–20124 Milano*

In France: Please write to *Penguin France S. A., 17 rue Lejeune, F–31000 Toulouse*

In Japan: Please write to *Penguin Books Japan, Ishikiribashi Building, 2–5–4, Suido, Tokyo 112*

In Greece: Please write to *Penguin Hellas Ltd, Dimocritou 3, GR–106 71 Athens*

In South Africa: Please write to *Longman Penguin Southern Africa (Pty) Ltd, Private Bag X08, Bertsham 2013*

READ MORE IN PENGUIN

A SELECTION OF POETRY

American Verse
British Poetry Since 1945
Caribbean Verse in English
Contemporary American Poetry
Contemporary British Poetry
English Poetry 1918–60
English Romantic Verse
English Verse
First World War Poetry
German Verse
Greek Verse
Irish Verse
Japanese Verse
Love Poetry
The Metaphysical Poets
Modern African Poetry
New Poetry
Poetry of the Thirties
Scottish Verse
Spanish Verse
Women Poets